ROUGH & TUMBLE

COMING HOME TO THE MOUNTAIN

FRANKIE LOVE

COPYRIGHT

Edited by Happily Ever Author
Proofread by Norma's Nook Proofreading
Cover Design by Cormar Covers
Map Illustration by Joel Kimmel
Map Typography by Andre Mora

HOME VALLEY

1 BARTLETT'S CABIN
2 ROUGH VALLEY FAMILY HUNTING CABIN
3 RYE'S CABIN
4 GRAHAM'S CABIN
5 RED AND ANNIE'S HOMESTEAD
6 REUBEN AND PLUM'S CABIN

HOME
WASHINGTON · EST. 1910

ROUGH VALLEY

7 CARTER'S CABIN
8 ROUGH FAMILY LAKE HOUSE
9 CASH'S RANCH HOUSE
10 BURLY FAIRGROUNDS
11 ROWDY FAMILY BARN
12 WOODY'S SHACK
13 WILLIAMS' FARM HOUSE
14 ANGUS'S CABIN

BURLY
WASHINGTON · EST. 1910

BOOK STORE

MYSTIC SHOP

BARBERSHOP

SNUG STREET

TENDER TRAIL

TOY STORE

HOME FOR CHRISTMAS

HAMMER HOME HARDWARE

HOME BREW

TREAT CANDY SHOP

HOME MADE BAKERY

HOME SLICE PIZZA

CLOTHING BOUTIQUE

HOME RUN SPORTS

NESTED HOME DECOR

HOMEWARD BOUND OUTDOOR GEAR

HOME GROWN NURSERY

RESTFUL ROAD

COZY COURT

DELIGHTFUL DRIVE

HOMER HERITAGE PARK

HOME HISTORY MUSEUM

TOWN HALL

HOME & HEART FURNITURE

MECHANIC

ANNABELL ROUGH ELEMENTARY

HOME COOKIN' DINER

POLICE DEPT

FEED STORE

FIRE DEPT

GENTLE GROVE

LEMON ROUGH'S COTTAGE

HOME AWAY FROM HOME B&B

BANK

HOME SICK URGENT CARE

HOME

WASHINGTON · EST. 1910

1

BARTLETT

I FELL IN LOVE ONCE, and it was with a girl named Plum. When I met her for the first time, it was the head-over-heels, dumbstruck, can't think of what to say kind of smitten.

She was 6 pounds, 4 ounces, surrounded by every living member of the Rough family, and there wasn't a dry eye in that hospital room.

Now, at five years old, my niece Plum is the center of my family. As she bounds into my hardware store, Hammer Home, the bells on the front door ring and a smile spreads across my face. I may try to play the part of a grumpy mountain man, but when that sweet pea comes to my register, looking for a lollipop, I melt.

"Uncle Bart, can I have a cherry one, pretty please?" she asks, her dark brown hair in pigtails to her waist, freckles across the bridge of her nose. She isn't wearing her winter coat and it's thirty degrees out.

"Who's supposed to be watching you right now?" I ask, thinking they're doing a piss-poor job at it as I hand her the requested sucker from the jar next to my register.

"Auntie Lemon, but she's on the phone with a client and so I snuck out."

"She's gonna be sour when she finds you missing, you know that, right?" I ask. My younger sister Lemon works above me in the main offices of our family's construction company, Rough House.

"Plum?" Lemon yanks open the front doors and calls for our niece, holding a child-size winter coat in hand. "Plum, I swear if you've–"

"She's right here," I say as Lemon walks toward us, hands on her hips. She's two years younger than me, but way more tightly wound. "Oops," I whisper to Plum. "You're busted."

"If you catch a cold before Grandma's Sunday dinner, I'll be the one who's blamed. You need to wear a coat. Not to mention you can't run out on me! It's dangerous to leave without an adult."

Even Plum seems to know this is a bit of a stretch. The three of us turn to look out the big shop window, taking in the quiet view. Hammer Home is nestled on Cozy Court, and there is virtually no crime in this town. There's a reason locals stay forever.

But as we look out the window at the picturesque street with the winter flower boxes filled, the bakery across the street with customers milling about, and families out doing weekend errands, I notice one thing out of place.

"Do you know whose dog that is?" I ask as a mangy mutt walks into a metal trash can, then a moment later, into a lamp post.

"Never seen it before," Lemon says, frowning.

I've already moved to the front door and opened it, concerned. The poor dog is clearly confused. As I cross the street, I wave to Nancy, who owns Home for Christmas, the holiday decor shop across the street. "Have you seen this dog's owner?" I ask her.

She shakes her head. "No, but I came out here because I was worried it would wander into the road."

I kneel down, Plum and Lemon at my side, and take a closer look at the pup. It is a small white dog with a black patch over its left eye. But both eyes are clouded over. "I think this mutt is blind," I say as he begins licking the back of my hand. "Sure is friendly though."

"And cute!" Plum says.

The dog is wearing a leather collar and it has a

bronze tag attached. "Hijinx," I read aloud. "Blind and Beloved."

"Does it list a phone number?" Lemon asks.

"Yep." I scoop up the pup and carry him across the street to the hardware store.

On a mission, Lemon and Plum find a bag of dog food, treats, and bowls for Hijinx as I call the number on his collar. "No answer and it says the voicemail box is full," I say. "Well, that's a bummer."

"The owner must be close by," Lemon says. "Call Graham at the police station and tell him you found a dog in case anyone calls looking for one."

"Shouldn't you be the one calling the station? Derek works there too," I joke, remembering how the local officer had a crush on my sister in high school. Our brother Graham is a cop, and I can call him directly, but I can't help giving my sister a hard time any chance I get.

"You want to go there?" Lemon's eyes light up. She loves nothing more than to bother me about my lack of a love life. "I heard Claudine and Tabitha over at the hair salon gossiping about you last week. Claudine's daughter is coming to town, and she wants to set you up."

"Oh god," I groan. Plum giggles though, and I pick that sweetheart up, twirling her around. "Why do I need a girl when I got one right here?"

Plum laughs. "You need to get married, Uncle Bart! And have babies so I can have cousins! I need kids to play with already!"

"She has a point," Lemon says with a smirk.

I roll my eyes. "Then get on it, Miss Lemon."

She laughs tight and high. "Right, because it's so easy to date when I have five brothers who have opinions on every single man in this town." She pulls out her phone, though, and types out a message. "I let Derek know you found a stray dog. I may not be interested in the man, but I am a decent human." She smirks, tucking her phone back in her pocket.

I run a hand over my jaw. Truth is, there isn't a guy who is good enough for my little sister. She may be a little high-strung, but she's smart as a whip and has a big heart – hell, it's her day off and she's babysitting our brother Reuben's daughter.

"Anyways... Plum, you ready to go?" Lemon turns to me. "We'll see you later tonight, right?"

"Mom wouldn't let me miss it," I joke as a couple enters the store with a shopping list in hand.

The girls leave and I help my customers, Hijinx snuggled on a blanket under my register. I keep looking out the window, distracted, wondering where the owner is. When I turn off the lights and flip my Open sign to Closed, I decide to take a leash off a display and clip it to Hijinx's collar. With a paper bag filled with doggy essentials, I turn my back to the street and lock up for the night.

It's only then I hear a woman shouting.

I turn, taking in the most beautiful woman I've ever seen in my life. Blonde hair whipping in the wind, dark eyes fixed on me. A figure that has my whole body aching for a future I never even considered before this very moment. Her. Me. Together.

But she isn't staring at me the way I'm staring at her.

She's glaring, really, and the shouting? Well, it's directed at me.

Accusing me of something. I try to focus on her words, but it's hard because her pink lips have me distracted as hell.

"Hey. You!" she shouts again, this time a few feet in front of me. "Are you trying to steal my dog?"

2

ABBY

HE'S A BIG GUY. Huge compared to me. Six foot three, broad shoulders, tough – and I'm nothing. Five-three with shoes. And I feel like this man could pick me up and throw me over his shoulder and, well, it sorta terrifies me. Reminds me of Ricky, if I'm being completely honest.

And I don't want to think about Ricky. Not now. Not ever again. I just want Hijinx back.

"That's my dog," I shout, stepping toward the big, rugged man, knowing he is the only thing standing between me and the love of my life.

His chocolate brown eyes widen as he takes me in. "I didn't take your dog."

"Hijinx," I say, "Mama's here." The sound of my voice has him perking right up, and I get down on my knees, and he bounces right over to me, yanking on the leash that the man holds. I pull it from his hand and he lets go.

"You know, you really shouldn't let your dog run around free. He could have gotten hit. I found him out in the street, running into the trash can. He could have hurt himself."

I stand with Hijinx in my arms, nuzzling him and holding him against my chest. "It's not like it was intentional." I shake my head. This man has no idea what I've been through today. Like I would ever do anything to part ways with Hijinx on purpose. This dog, he's my whole world, now more than ever.

"Well, he's been here with me at the hardware store for the last three hours, and no one came looking."

I blink back tears that I hate to have brimming in my eyes. "Sorry," I say. "I had to go to Urgent Care. I would've kept looking, but..."

"Are you okay?" He instantly softens.

"I'm fine." I say. "Just... It's nothing."

"What happened to you?"

"I'm telling you, it's fine, okay?" I'm defensive. I always am. On guard, looking out for myself, because there's never been anyone else looking out for me. "Well, thanks for finding him. And keeping him safe. Sorry for yelling at you. I was just scared."

"It's okay." He runs a hand over his beard. "I

shouldn't have yelled at you either, or assumed you weren't looking for your dog. I tried to call your number, but there wasn't any answer."

I lick my lips. "Yeah, my phone's not working."

"I'm Bartlett Rough," he tells me. "Are you new in town? I've never seen you before."

"I'm Abby," I tell him, "and yeah, I just got into Home this morning." I see him looking up and down the street, probably wondering if I have a car. I shake my head, explaining, "I came in on the train."

He gives me a half smile. "What are you, in some Jack Kerouac novel?"

I laugh at that. Surprised actually, maybe, that he knows Jack Kerouac, that he reads. I don't know. That all sounds ridiculous, now that I think it. I know nothing about this man.

He works at a hardware store and he took care of my dog and he is big and strong and handsome, and he fills out that winter coat very well. And he apologized. All those things are better than the things I know about most of the men I've met in my life.

"Years ago, I came through this town with my family. And I thought it was the best place in the whole world. I always thought I would come back here one day, if I got a chance, if I could get away." I shrug, and as I do, Hijinx wriggles in my arms, causing the bandages on my arm to pull, making me wince in pain and set him down.

"Are you all right?"

"It's okay." I set Hijinx down, holding his leash tight. "It's just..." I press a hand to my stomach. "It's going to sound crazy, but when I was getting off the train, these guys stole my wallet, and I tried to get it back, which was probably stupid because they were two men and they were bigger than me. And I got sliced by their knife."

"What? Shit." Bartlett shakes his head. "I didn't know people were getting in knife fights in Home."

"That's why I was at Urgent Care. I got stitches."

"Where?" he asks, worry in his voice.

"It's not so bad," I say. But he is already stepping closer, listening with care, concern in his eyes.

I unzip my winter coat, shove off the sleeve, then pull up the cuff of my sweater, showing him the bandage. "Six stitches." I shake my head. I shove down the sweater sleeve, zipping my winter coat.

"You've had a hell of a day," Bartlett says.

I laugh tightly. "I've had hell of a life."

"What are you doing now?" he asks. "It's about dinner time."

"Now? I was going to go to the Home Away

From Home Bed and Breakfast and see if I could get a room."

"Without your wallet?" he asks. "Not to be too personal, but do you have any money?"

Bartlett clearly is worried for me and my fear dissolves in his presence. For the first time in days, I feel myself relax. A man I just met, who rescued my dog, is making me calm in a way I rarely am.

"They ditched my wallet after taking my cash, but thankfully I have my credit card in my backpack. I still need to go to the police station to get it. The doctor at Homesick Urgent Care told me the clinic would get me a room, though. He felt terrible for what happened. Graham, the police officer who came to take a report, doesn't think the men who jumped me are from here."

"Well, to be fair, it wasn't technically Home where you got attacked. The train station is on the outskirts of town, closer to Burly. Still, this is the worst welcome back to Home I've ever heard of."

I shrug. "It could be worse," I say, "I mean, what if I hadn't found Hijinx tonight? What if you had just taken him with you, and I was here by myself without my dog, and I thought I had lost him?"

Bartlett groans. "You're right. It could have been worse. Still, damn, you got cut by some hoodlums from Burly the same day you rode in on a train, after running away from some life that doesn't sound like it was all that good."

I run a hand through my hair, smiling shyly. "You said something about dinner?"

Bartlett laughs. "Yeah. I think taking you home for dinner would be a way to make up for your bad first impression."

I shake my head. "It wasn't the first impression. My first impression was incredible. It was the summer I turned ten and I came here with my family for the circus, and it was..."

Bartlett cuts me off. "I remember the circus. Ah, that was amazing. I was 14 that summer. Oh my God, my sister Lemon, she thought she was going to be an acrobat after that circus came through town. I swear to God, my brothers and sisters and me, we spent the rest of that summer doing all sorts of acrobatic shit. And my mom and dad told us if one of us broke a bone, they weren't going to pay for the medical bills; we'd have to use the money in our piggy banks."

I laugh. "Really? That's hilarious." I realize he has no idea what I meant when I said I *came for the circus*, because my whole family was, *is,* the traveling circus, but I'm not going to get into that here. Right now, this man who saved my dog is looking at me like I am someone worth seeing, and I've never felt like that before.

When you spend your whole life on the road, you never stick around anywhere long enough to find out what it's like to be at home.

This man has asked me to come with him to dinner. I'm not missing a hot meal.

"So, where is this dinner?" I ask, realizing I can't just go to some stranger's house. Maybe we can go to a restaurant in town. I know I don't want this conversation to end.

"Oh, well, first of all, you don't need to be nervous about heading somewhere alone with a guy you just met. That officer who helped you today, Graham? He's my brother. And he'll be there. And so will the rest of my family." He gives me a sheepish grin. "At my parents' house. Every Sunday night, no questions asked, we all have to come back for dinner. My mom, she'll kill us if we all don't make it."

My eyes widen. "And how many brothers and sisters do you have?"

"Six," he says, "but don't worry. No one will give you a hard time."

"And how can you be so sure about that?" I ask.

He smiles, "Oh, because all eyes are going to be on Fig tonight."

"Fig?" I ask.

He nods, "Yeah. She's the littlest sister, and she's trying to convince my parents that she should spend the last semester of her senior year abroad. So, that's what the conversation will be about tonight. Her pitching a fit. So no worries, Abby, you've just got to sit back, eat my mama's good food, and relax."

I smile. "Hijinx is welcome?"

He nods. "More than welcome." He bends down and picks him up, and then he takes my hand.

"Welcome to Home, properly this time." He leans in close, and for a moment, I have a crazy thought that this man I've just met might kiss me.

He doesn't, of course, but if he had?

I swallow. Honestly, I think I would've loved it.

3

BARTLETT

DRIVING UP TO MY PARENTS' house, I look over at Abby, this wild-haired girl with eyes filled with a faraway look, her dog in her lap, a backpack at her feet. She's seen things, been places.

I don't know if she's been traveling a long time, but she looks tired. She says she was meaning to come home, but I want to know where she comes from.

Though, before I can get to that, I figure I better prepare her for what's coming right now.

I clear my throat. "The thing is," I say. "My family–"

"It's a big one, right? You have a little sister, Fig?" she asks.

"Right," I say, "she's just turned eighteen."

"Okay," Abby says, nodding and taking it in.

"And she's a senior in high school," I say. "We all went to school here at the Home Secondary School." I shrug. "I'm not sure what kind of high school you went to, but this school, it's small. Everybody knows each other. This whole town is small."

She gives a smile that lights up the car, which is saying something considering the sun has already set and we're driving up the big old mountain road, the pine trees crowding out the black sky full of stars. Her smile makes anything seem possible.

"I was homeschooled," she says. "We were on the road a lot."

I chuckle. "Well, we were certainly not homeschooled. My mom wanted us out of the house so she could have some peace and quiet for seven hours a day. God knows she needed it."

"So how many brothers do you have exactly?" Abby asks.

"There are seven of us in all. Five boys, two girls."

"Where are you in the lineup?" she asks.

"I'm second-in-command. My brother Rye, he's a few years older. I'm 26. How old are you?"

"Twenty-one." She twists her lip. "So you got a big old family, a mother who somehow managed all of you, and a little sister who is ready to go spread her wings. Okay. Should I know anything else before we go to this family dinner?"

"Have you been to many family dinners?" I ask.

"Family dinners?" Abby repeats. "Well, my family was pretty close growing up. I mean, they are still close." Her words falter a bit.

"But you're not with them. Do they know where you are?"

"No, not exactly. I needed some space is all," Abby says, her fingers fidgeting, running along the hem of her jacket. "I needed to clear my head. I needed to spread my wings. Maybe I'm like Fig."

Laughing, I look over at her. "You're not like Fig."

"I don't know if that's a good thing or a bad thing," Abby says, laughing. Her laugh, it's a good one. Big and bright.

Our eyes catch. "I love Fig to death, but she's a little spoiled, being the baby and all. You don't seem spoiled. You seem like your head's on straight. Like you've been through some shit and you're not taking any of it for granted."

"Guess that's not the worst assessment of me considering we just met," Abby says, "and you seem like you'd be the oldest brother considering you run a hardware store. You're so responsible that you take in stray dogs and girls."

Now it's my turn to smile. I want to reach for

her hand. I want to hold it. I want to do more than hold it. I want to hold *her*. Hug her, take care of her. She seems lost, but not in a fragile, breakable way. She seems lost in a way that says she really does need to come home, here.

"Rye is certainly the oldest. You'll know that when you meet him, but he is different than me. He's an ass, if I'm going to say it bluntly. Me? I'm the nice guy. The guy who plays it safe. Who always does what he's told and who makes his mama happy."

"Ah, I see. You're a mama's boy," Abby teases.

"Hey," I say, pulling up to the big old house where I was raised. Abby's eyes widen as she takes it in. The house is huge. "My parents own a construction company called Rough House," I clarify. "My hardware store, Hammer Home, was my dad's shop for years, and their office is above my store. They build custom homes all over the mountainside. My dad built this home with his own two hands."

"It's incredible," Abby says.

The headlights on my truck show off every big bay window of the two-story house, with attic rooms. There's a big barn and a garage with a rec room over the three bays.

I open my car door and jog around to open hers. "I'd say, for being the Rough family, we're pretty gentle, but I wouldn't want that rumor to spread."

"Says the mama's boy," Abby teases.

I take Hijinx from her and hold him in my arms, not wanting her bandages to tear. "You okay?" I ask.

She nods. "Yeah. I mean, I have no idea what I'm in for, but I appreciate the invitation."

"It would have been terrible for you to go eat by yourself at the diner tonight."

"I've eaten plenty of meals alone."

"I thought you did a bunch of things with your family?" I ask, looking for clarification, trying to understand what Abby's life is really like.

"Yeah, I did. But you know how you can be with people and still feel really alone?"

I shake my head. "Actually, no, I've never felt like that."

Abby's lips twist into something wistful. "You're lucky, Bartlett," she says. "And right now, I feel pretty lucky to be here with you."

Walking inside the house, I'm suddenly nervous. I've never brought a woman home – and I have this deep need for my family to like Abby. To love her. She looks over at me as I close the heavy front door, and we stand in the big foyer, alone for a moment. A rare quiet moment in this loud, rambunctious house. There is a big staircase leading upstairs to the bedrooms, a hall leading to the kitchen and my dad's den. To the left are the big family and dining rooms.

But the foyer is filled with shoes and coats, a closet overflowing with decades of hunting jackets and rain boots, clogs and sweaters. I watch as Abby takes it all in.

"This feels like a real home," she whispers as we both slide off our shoes, adding them to the pile by the door.

I take her hand protectively. "You okay?"

She nods, but I know there is a well of emotion in her eyes as we walk into the family room, together, where my entire family is gathered.

Watching through her eyes, as she takes in the family photos hanging on every square inch of the walls, I see the house in a new light. The warm wood finishes my father added, the wicker baskets filled with the books my mom is reading next to her favorite chair. The basket of yarn and knitting needles for when Grandma Rosie comes over, the blazing fire warming the room, the chess match on the coffee table between Graham and Mac. Fig braiding Plum's hair. My mom calling for Rye to grab some cans of chicken stock from the pantry. Lemon showing Dad how to download some app on his phone.

No one notices us for a moment, and time

seems to still. My hand's in Abby's, hers squeezing mine right back, and suddenly I don't feel like I'm bringing home a stranger for dinner. I feel like I am bringing home Abby. My Abby.

Eventually Fig notices us, and all eyes turn to the newcomer. I introduce Abby to my parents. "This is Redford. And my mom, Anise."

My dad chuckles. "You can call me Red. And this is Annie," he says. "And you're Abby?"

After I explain how we came to meet this afternoon, my siblings all chime in with welcomes and introductions of their own. My niece Plum is thrilled with the prospect of a new dog.

"Well, I already met him," Plum explains to Abby. "We found him on the street. We were so scared because your poor puppy seemed so sad. But then Uncle Bartlett brought him into the shop and I got him this leash and Uncle Bart, he let me pick it. What do you think of the color? I chose purple because I thought purple would look really pretty with his fur."

"I think purple is a lovely color, and thank you for helping with Hijinx," Abby says with a grin. She takes off her jacket, and my sister Lemon hangs it up on a coat rack for her.

Fig is twirling her hair and showing off pamphlets on France to anyone who will listen. I hear her travel pitch in the background. "It's only four months and it is mostly in Paris. I would be getting the education of a lifetime. And considering I took two years of French already, I'm basically completely prepared." Fig talks with her hands, her long black hair swinging around her shoulders as she tries to get everyone's attention with her new plan.

I know there's no way in hell my mother's going to let her out of her sight. She's not just Mom's baby. We all see her as ours to protect.

Hijinx is happy, and Abby is holding her own with Lemon and my dad, and I'm listening to Mac tell Graham about the building plans for some country lodge he's working on over in the Burly Mountains.

"I just don't understand why you would want to clear-cut so many trees," Graham says adamantly.

"This acreage is prime real estate though!" Mac debates. "The future is now! Uncle Luke agreed with me." Not wanting to listen to that discussion right now, I wind through the house.

I find Rye in the kitchen. The fridge is open and he's rooting around for a beer. "Want one?" he asks.

"Sure," I say.

"So who's that girl?"

"You heard how we met?"

"Sure," he says, eyes narrowing. "But what do you know about her?"

"What do you care? You think she's gonna steal my wallet?" When Rye doesn't answer, I snort. "How are you always such a cynic?"

"Uh. Why wouldn't I be?"

"Maybe because the world's not actually out to get us?" I say, rolling my eyes as I pop open the cold one.

Rye takes a slug of his beer. He looks like he hasn't slept in days. The guy is a train wreck.

He needs someone nice in his life, or maybe a dog, a dog like Hijinx. Someone to soften his rough edges. He shakes his head, looking pissed.

"Did I do something to offend you?" I ask with a growing growl.

"I just think it's weird that you brought some girl home to Sunday dinner. We don't even know her."

"Rye, it's dinner," I say. "She's new to town. She was held up by a knife earlier this afternoon."

Rye's jaw tenses at that, his mood shifting. "Fuck, you serious?"

"Abby got stitches for what they did to her. Poor thing had her wallet stolen."

Now Rye is more than pissed. "I bet it was those guys in Burly. They've been causing lots of problems. It's time they slow their goddamn roll. Don't you think?"

"Yeah I do. But I don't even know who did it.

We should go talk to Graham at the police department and find out."

Rye nods. "Yeah, we should. And look, I'm not saying she shouldn't be here. I'm just wondering who she is."

"Well, it's nice that you're protective," I say, "but she's my date tonight. Okay? So let me do the protecting when it comes to Abby."

"All right." Rye runs a hand over his beard. "Enough said."

"Good," I say as Lemon comes into the kitchen with Abby at her side.

"What are you grumpy boys talking about?" she asks with a deepening frown on her face.

"I swear, the two of you," I say, pointing to Rye and then Lemon, "are both constantly so irritable." I walk out of the room, taking Abby's hand as I do.

Abby asks me what that was all about.

"Honestly, I think they both need to find someone to date and get laid."

She laughs then leans in close, her warm breath on my ear. "And what about you, Bartlett? Do you need to get laid?"

I groan. "You trying to drive me wild before we sit down to Sunday supper?"

She bites her lip. "Now that you've mentioned it, it could be something we continue talking about when we're not about to sit down at the dinner table with your parents."

She points to the room full of my family, a few feet away.

I grin. But my hand is suddenly at her waist and she is at my side. "I'm happy you're here," I say, standing close to her, feeling her warmth. I realize I like this girl. I like the way she smiles and laughs. The way she's comfortable in her own skin and the way she entered this big, wild house without cowering in the corner. She was just here, talking to Plum and my parents and me like she's been here all along.

"What are you thinking?" she asks.

"I'm thinking I'm really glad you came home."

4

_____

ABBY

WHEN WE DRIVE down the Rough Mountains, back into town, Bartlett reaches over and takes my hand in his. The feeling is electric.

I'm not alone in that.

He looks over at me, his other hand still on the wheel. He groans, "How have I been living my whole life without knowing you?"

There's a drawl to his voice, and he may not live in the country, but he still lives far from any big city. Far from skyscrapers and towering complexes. He is a small-town guy, through and through, with a family who understands the true meaning of family. I don't think he has any idea how lucky he is.

"So, your family is pretty special," I tell him.

"They didn't scare you away? I know the questions at dinner got a little intense."

"Nobody asked me anything that I couldn't answer."

The questions were pretty simple. What do I like to do for fun? Do I have a favorite movie? What's the last book I read? It was like they'd all been prepped on how to ask appropriate questions that didn't press too hard, too fast. I appreciated it. Someone in their family along the way got the memo that religion and politics were off limits. And also, any visitor's history might be a little too much, too soon, because they didn't go into those kinds of details. Didn't ask why I was all alone with my dog Hijinx and a backpack and nothing else to my name. They didn't ask things I wasn't ready to answer.

Maybe Bartlett gave them a heads up that I'd had a hard day. And if so, I'm more smitten with him than ever, but maybe they're simply good people who have decency and respect and boundaries.

Regardless, that dinner was maybe the best dinner of my life. And it had nothing to do with the home-cooked food that Annie made, which was incredible: meatloaf, mashed potatoes, green peas, iced tea, pound cake with homemade whipped cream for dessert. Heavenly. Ten out of ten.

"You were right," I tell Bartlett. "All eyes were

on Fig." That girl, she was determined to get her way.

"Oh man. She was so mad though. Leaving the dinner table in a puddle of tears is not a happy way to go," he says.

"Do you think she'll get over it quickly?" I ask, having no idea how families like his resolve conflict. In my family, it was yelling, fighting, and one-word answers. That's why I was kept for so long. I wasn't in a cage like the elephants and the tigers, though I felt like it. I wasn't allowed out.

That's why I ran. I felt like I had no choice.

"Oh, Fig will come around. My mom will promise her fabric for some fancy dress for prom and Fig will be happy as a clam sewing it. Eventually Fig will realize that college will be a better time for her to travel to Europe."

"It sounds like your parents are pretty supportive of all of you."

"Yeah. I just think it's a new thing because the rest of us, we never really wanted to go all that far. We really never wanted to leave home. Fig, she's been itching to go since she was little. And I think the reality of that is going to catch up to my mom and my dad pretty quick."

"Do you have other family around here?" I ask him.

"Oh, for sure. My dad's parents live in town and

then my mom's family, they live in Burly, the Rowdy family. My uncle Angus and his boys."

"Wow," I say. "It's pretty much a whole family tree right here in this valley."

"Does that scare you? The idea of a man like me never wanting to leave?"

I shake my head. "Not at all. I find it very comforting. I've spent so much of my life on the road. The idea of being settled somewhere, someone wanting to be settled? I like that about you, Bartlett."

He laces his fingers through mine tightly as we pull up to the bed and breakfast. "I'll come in with you just to make sure you get checked in, all right?"

"Thanks," I say. "I really appreciate it."

Bartlett tells me his sister Lemon lives right next door.

"Really?" I say. "That's a really cute place."

"Yeah. It was a real fixer-upper, but, well, she had plenty of brothers to help her fix it up."

We go inside the main office and it's a quaint, charming building in town. I smile as we walk to the front desk.

"Bart, what are you doing in here on a Sunday night? I'd expect your mama wants you home for dinner," the older woman at the desk scolds.

"We just finished dinner," he says. "Mary, this is Abby. She's got a room here from the doctor over at

Homesick Urgent Care. At least that's what we're hoping."

"Oh yes, he called over earlier. I'm so sorry, Abby. I heard what happened to you this afternoon. I can't believe that. I was just shocked."

"I'm okay," I say, "I'm just glad that there was a room at all."

Mary's eyes run over me, though. Landing on Hijinx. "Um, is that your dog?" She reaches for a tissue and blows her nose.

"Yeah. This is Hijinx. He comes with me. We're a package deal."

Mary blows her nose loudly, pointing to a sign. "I'm so sorry, but we have a no pets policy here at the Home Away From Home Bed and Breakfast. I'm really sorry. But I'm very allergic and so is my husband."

"I'm so sorry. I didn't realize. I'd never want to hurt you or get you sick. Is there another hotel in town?"

Mary looks over at Bart. "In Burly there's a motel."

"I can't have her go there," Bartlett says.

"Of course not." Mary shakes her head, sneezing again. I back away with my dog, my stomach dropping, not knowing what I'm going to do.

Bartlett runs a hand over his beard. "We're just

going to go outside and talk, Mary."

"All right. Of course. I'm so sorry. Again. I really am. I didn't know you had a pet with you." She blows her nose loudly into her tissue.

As we walk outside, tears well up in my eyes. "I can go to the police station," I tell Bartlett. "And get my wallet now. And I can get a taxi to the motel or you could take me. I just–"

"Hey." Bartlett runs a hand over my shoulder. "You know, I could keep Hijinx for the night."

I bite my bottom lip. Hijinx is my constant, and not being with him feels scariest of all. Bartlett must sense this because he wraps me up in a warm hug.

"Hey. Why don't you just stay with me tonight? I mean, not to be presumptuous. And you can say no, if you want. I can take you over to the motel. Of course, it's just, well, it's not the nicest place. And you've already had one hell of a day. I have an extra bedroom at my cabin. It's nothing fancy. It's not like my parents' house, but if you want to stay with me, of course I'd have you and Hijinx. I'm not allergic to him."

"Really?" I ask. "You wouldn't mind?"

"Don't say another word." He gives me a smile that melts my weary heart, and then he jogs inside to tell Mary that I'm not going to be staying there at all tonight.

A moment later, we're back in his truck driving up Rough Mountain once again. But this time we turn left towards his place on the edge of Rough River on the left side of town. When we park in front of his cabin, he grabs my backpack and Hijinx. Then he unlocks the door and pushes it open for me.

Before flipping on the lights, he says his cabin is nothing special, but he's being modest which shouldn't surprise me.

It's a lovely cabin. It's rough and wild, just like him. "I felled all the trees myself for this place," he says. "I wanted it to feel rustic but still cozy. I know some people like a little bit more of a *house* house, but I wanted to feel like I was in a cabin in the woods." He shakes his head, running a hand through his hair. "Does that sound weird?"

"No, it sounds like you're a real mountain man," I say with a grin.

"You like that?" he asks me. "Mountain men?"

"I like you," I say.

He sets Hijinx down and heads to the kitchen to fill up a bowl of water for him. Looking around, I see the floor plan is open. There is a hall down to the left with a few doors, the bathroom and bedrooms, I assume. And then there's a big open living room, dining room, and kitchen. There's a loft above, and looking up, there's a big light fixture full of antlers.

All the furniture is covered with plaid, red and forest green. I smile, thinking how wonderful this cabin would be at the holidays.

Bartlett comes toward me a moment later, asking if I'm thirsty or hungry.

"No, I don't think I could eat another thing after that meal at your mom's house."

"Me too," he says. "Well, then, I can show you the bedrooms. I don't know if you want to shower."

I swallow, thinking of what I really want. Him, him, him.

I follow Bartlett down the hall, and he pushes open one bedroom door, then another. They're nice. One is set up as an office. And another one is a guest room. The third room is his. It has a big bed and a nice, masculine dresser.

Everything is just so put together and orderly. Nice. Clean. My eyes flit around the surfaces, taking it all in.

"Where are you?" he asks. "I feel like I lost you somewhere from the car to the house."

"I just am trying to put you together. I'm wondering, how are you single?" I ask. "You seem so perfect."

He groans. "You know, I've heard that my whole life. Bartlett, you know, it's a kind of pear. So people always said, you're gonna find a girl one day and you're going to make the perfect pair. It's a lot of pressure."

"Pressure to look for your perfect pair?" I ask him.

"More like pressure to find the perfect girl."

"That makes sense. I mean, with a family like you have, I can see how there would be pressure to live up to their expectations."

"Well, it's not just that I want my family to approve. I put high expectations on myself."

I nod slowly, running my hand over the top of his walnut dresser. "So you're looking for a certain kind of woman, and until you meet her, you'll be alone in this perfect house, this perfect cabin, with the perfect job and nearly the perfect life?"

"When you say it like that, I kind of sound like a dick, don't I?"

"I don't think so. Like I said, you're pretty lucky."

"What about you, Abby? Why are you single?"

"Me?" I let out a sigh. "I'm single because I could not imagine spending a life with the guy my parents picked for me. He was the kind of man who made you feel small when you just wanted to be yourself. The kind of man who made me feel weak, even when I felt strong. I couldn't be with a man like that. And my parents wouldn't listen to me when I told them. But that is a story for another day." I shrug. "So, what is your idea of perfection, Bartlett?"

"What is perfect to me? Well, I read a book on the laws of attraction. You know about it?"

"Tell me," I say.

"Well, one of the laws of attraction is believing that the present is perfect."

"The present is perfect?" I twist my lips. "That seems like a pretty hard law to practice."

"What if it wasn't?" he presses. "What if we just chose to believe it all the time? Right now?"

I smile. "Well, *this* present seems pretty near perfect."

"It does, doesn't it? This whole day has, actually – minus the knifing."

I laugh, closing my eyes and shaking my head as Bartlett steps closer to me. "The moment I saw you, I felt like it was perfect. Your smile. Your eyes. The way you looked at me with such anger thinking I had stolen your dog. Like I was a dognapper." Bartlett grins. "Sure, maybe I wasn't thinking straight because it was cold as balls outside. That January freeze was setting in. But I don't think it was the frost in the air. I think... I think something else was sweeping through town. I think that was you."

I shake my head. "Stop it," I say, pressing my

hand to his chest.

But he sets his hands on my waist. "No, I won't stop. I'm thinking maybe you haven't heard just how good you are. Maybe you spent your life hearing other kinds of things, other stories about yourself, and maybe it's time you heard something new."

I take in a slow breath. Then I let it out. I listen.

"Because Abby, you make me really happy. Today at my parents' house, I felt really good. And it wasn't because the meatloaf was amazing, which it was. And it wasn't because Plum was cute as hell, which she is. And it wasn't because I like listening to my siblings argue, which can be entertaining. It was because you were there next to me. There's a groundedness you've got that I am drawn to. I can't get enough of it."

"You mean all that? After one afternoon with me, a girl you just met who came into town on a train?"

"I think you're a girl who reads Jack Kerouac. And I'm a guy who does too. And I think that means we might both be onto something here."

"The present is perfect," I tell him.

And then he kisses me and kisses me and kisses me.

My lips part, and God, I hope this man kisses me forever.

5

BARTLETT

HER LIPS ARE SOFT, willing. Smooth. And damn, I don't want this kiss to end. Her eyes flutter open, and her fingers run through my hair. She smiles in my arms and I know I'm holding her tight.

I don't wanna let her go. She's someone I've just met and I'm probably breaking 1000 rules.

It's reckless and it's ridiculous. It's also fucking happening. This woman and me, tonight? It's fucking on. There's a hunger in her eyes, and there's a need in my cock, and there's more than that. There was a connection in the car that whole drive up to my cabin.

"What are you thinking?" she asks me.

"I'm thinking I want you in that bed. Now."

"I've never done this," she says, her eyes exploring mine.

"Never ever?"

"Never ever. But that doesn't mean I don't want to," she says softly. She licks her lips. Her tongue is pink.

Her innocence may not be on the surface, but I can see it now; it's a hidden layer she wasn't showing right away, but now that it's come out, I understand. She is tough on the outside. Soft in the center. And fuck, she's a virgin.

"I don't want to press you to do anything you're not ready to do. We just met. We don't need to have sex the first night."

Her hands press to my chest, fingering the buttons of my flannel shirt. She's licking her lips again. My cock is hard as a rock.

I want her in ways she doesn't even understand. "What if we just start something and see where it takes us?" she asks, her voice lifting at the end, trying to see where I might go with this.

She has no fucking clue that I will go wherever she wants to take me. Including to the ends of the goddamn earth, because I like her. I like her one hell of a lot. Abby is the kind of girl you fall for. Hard.

This girl with a blind dog who's come in on a fucking train, rolling into my life in a way I was not at all prepared for.

But I've been playing it safe for years, doing

what everyone expects – running the family store, showing up for Sunday dinner. When's the last time I had real fun? When's the last time I went for it? I've been waiting for perfection but what if the present really is perfect?

I run my hands over the hem of her shirt, lifting it up over her head. The bandage on her arm makes me wince.

"I hate that this happened to you," I say, running my fingers over the gauze.

"I hate that it did too," she says, giving me a half smile. "But look, right now, here we are. In this room. Together. I would've never imagined this."

Hijinx walks into the room, and he stumbles a bit until he curls up on the carpet next to the bed.

I run my hands over her bare back. "You okay?" I ask, my fingers on the clasp of her bra. She nods as she begins to unbutton my shirt.

I unclasp her bra, setting it on my bed then taking in the view of her naked chest.

"You're beautiful," I tell her. "I mean really fucking gorgeous."

Her cheeks turn pink and she shakes her head. "Stop it."

I kiss her cheek, her ears, her mouth. "You don't believe me?" I turn her around to face the mirror over my dresser. I wrap my arms around her belly, holding her tight. With her back to my chest, I know she can feel my cock against her ass, and I like that. I want her to feel my length, my desire.

She presses her ass tighter against me, leaning her head back against my chest as she takes us in through the mirror.

"Do you like what you see?" I ask.

"I love what I see," she says softly. "You and me, together... a perfect pair."

I turn her around so she's facing me, and I kiss her again. Hungry this time. Desperate. Massaging her breasts with a need she understands.

I want her desperately. I lower my mouth to her breast, her nipple against my tongue. I twirl it in my mouth, sucking her tits.

She moans against me, her hands in my hair, her need mounting as I draw her to the bed, careful of the wound on her arm but wanting so much to taste every inch of her body.

"Show me what it means to be taken by a real man?" she asks me.

I'm not sure if she's ready for everything but she's ready for something. I unzip her jeans and I tug them past her hips, shove her panties off too.

"I don't want to scare you, but I want you to know how badly I want to taste you. I want to lick you up and down, Abby. I want your creamy cunt against my mouth. Do you understand what I'm saying?"

She nods. "I want that too. I think I've had a stressful enough day. So an orgasm sounds pretty delicious."

I chuckle at her candor, her confidence. And then I take in that pussy. Because fuck – it's pink and tight, and damn...

Now *that* is perfection.

I spread her knees and I dip my mouth to her entrance, running my tongue over her sweet folds. "Just lie back and relax," I say. "Like you said, you've had a stressful enough day. How about you just enjoy yourself. Consider this your real *welcome home* gift."

She laughs, pressing her hand to her arm. "Don't make me laugh so hard. I don't think it's good for the stitches."

"I apologize, and fuck, I don't exactly want to talk right now. I have other things to do."

Abby's pussy is sweet and wet and so damn tight. My fingers ache to spread her lips nice and wide, to get her juices dripping. She deserves it. She deserves the fucking world after the day she had.

So I give her what she needs. I begin to finger her nice and slow, opening up her virgin hole, treating her the way she deserves to be treated.

Up and down, in and out, making her wet and making her mine.

"Oh fuck, oh yes, ohhhhhhhhhh......" She sits up, panting, her eyes wide, her voice tight. "Is this how it's supposed to go?"

"Yeah, baby," I say. "That's called a fucking orgasm."

"In that case, I've never actually had one before. Because that... This..." She runs a hand over her forehead. "Oh my God, Bart. Don't stop, don't, don't..."

I begin to finger her harder, faster, making her juicy come squirt against my mouth as I suck her clit. Her back arches and her fingers grope the sheets as she comes harder for me.

"Oh, oh God... Oh my God, Bartlett, come here... Come here, please, please..." she begs.

I do what she asks cause I'm not gonna fucking deny this woman a single fucking thing. I get in the bed with her, at her side, and she's reaching for the button of my jeans, forcing them down and reaching for my cock.

"We don't have to do this," I tell her. "We can take our time, Abby. There's no rush."

"I want it. My pussy wants it. I need you in me now."

Not wanting to deny her a goddamn thing, I take off my jeans and my boxers. And she takes my cock gingerly in her hand. I tell her to move her hand up and down, nice and slow.

"Like that?" she asks, eager to please.

"Just like that, baby," I tell her, running a hand over her bare back, her body so pure and naked, dripping with innocence and filled with desire.

I want to make her feel good but I also want to make her understand that this night is something special. She is something special to me.

"Hey," I say, taking a strand of hair behind her ear. "I know we just met, but I'm really glad we did."

"I'm glad we met too, Bart, but you don't have to tell me anything to make this feel less like... like a one-night stand."

I frown. "This isn't a one-night stand. I don't do that kind of thing. Ever."

"Really?" She shakes her head. "Never mind. I just want to be here now. Remember? The present is perfect."

But I don't like that. I shake my head. Sitting up in bed, drawing her into my lap, we're naked. My cock is hard; her pussy is wet and pulsing with need. Her tits are fucking gorgeous and everything about her turns me on.

But I need her to know something. I need her to know me.

"I'm not that guy. I know you just met me so you don't have to believe me, but I'm not. I've been celibate for ages. I don't hook up with people. I don't go on dates. Everyone in this town thinks I'm waiting for the perfect woman... maybe I was waiting for you."

"That's a lot to put on a woman you just met." Abby's eyes darken. "You don't even know me. I could be gone tomorrow. You don't know my last name or where I come from or what my family's like. I heard what your brother was saying about me; he wonders who I really am. And here you are confessing that you think maybe I'm *your person...* Bartlett, don't. We can have sex. I want to have sex for the first time with you because I've been waiting for someone like you. Someone kind and sweet and generous and handsome and loving, but... You don't need to make promises you aren't prepared to keep. We can just have fun. What if we just let that be enough?"

"I wish I were that kind of guy," I tell her, cupping her cheek and kissing her softly. "But I'm not. I can't do casual. I brought you to this bed and I sucked your clit like there was no tomorrow because hell, I was thinking that tomorrow you and I had a future. But..." I shake my head. "Maybe I'm a fool. Because... maybe you're not seeing things the same way as me."

Abby exhales slowly, running a hand over my beard and then through my hair. "I don't think it's that I don't see things the same way as you... It's just, your last name may be Rough, but it feels like your life's been pretty dang charmed. I'm the one who's had hard knocks forever. And a girl like me? Well, even if the present is perfect, deep down I don't think I'm good enough to be anyone's perfect pair."

6

ABBY

BARTLETT LOOKS at me like I completely ruined the mood, and I probably did.

"Say something," I groan. "Anything."

I'm sitting in this man's lap, this perfect specimen of a human being, telling him I'm not good enough to be with him.

After he's just offered me more than meaningless sex. What woman says no to that? Especially after he licked my pussy up and down until I literally came all over his face. And now I'm telling him no, actually I don't want your huge cock to fill my pussy until I orgasm all over you, even though I know that instead of being ghosted, I can count on you to call me the next day.

Smart move, Abby.

"I feel like you're trying to sabotage this before it's even started," he tells me.

"Wow, so you can see through my bullshit real fast," I say, dropping my face in my hands and rolling out of his lap. I stand on his wool rug, looking around for a robe to cover my naked body. I feel exposed, vulnerable, and stupid all at the same time.

He gets out of bed and hands me a flannel bathrobe that's hanging on the back of his door. "Here," he says, "put this on."

He pulls on a pair of gray sweats, which, okay, he looks freaking incredible in. His cock is still hard and he looks like my horniest dreams ever.

"How about we have a drink," he says. "I think the orgasm is messing with your mind."

"Ha ha," I say dryly. Though maybe he's onto something. He gave me a mind-blowing orgasm and I immediately tried to run away. Am I scared to feel that good more than once?

"Do you like chamomile or peppermint tea better?"

"Chamomile," I tell him. "And can I tell you how charming I find it that you're offering me tea instead of whiskey or vodka?"

"I'm not gonna get you drunk before I get you back in bed."

"Oh, so you're planning on getting me back in bed tonight?"

"Yeah," he says, wrapping his arms around me, lifting me up and carrying me into the kitchen. He sets me down on the counter and then he kisses me. Hard.

I open up. "Maybe I was trying to push you away before you had a chance to break my heart or something."

"Wow, so you think I'm heartbreak material?"

I bite my bottom lip. "You want me to be honest?"

"Brutally." Bartlett sets the tea kettle on his stove and finds two ceramic mugs, placing tea bags in them.

"I think you're the epitome of heartbreak material. I wasn't lying when I said all those nice things about you. You are handsome and kind and wonderful in ways I've never experienced before. Your family is lovely and your home is beautiful and–" Bartlett presses his lips to mine, kissing me hard, taking my breath away.

I wrap my arms around his neck, laughing against his mouth. "I guess that's one way to shut me up."

"That wasn't what I was trying to do. I just wanted to kiss you because fuck, I don't think I've ever had a woman say such nice things about me."

"I guess after I said all those things I immediately wondered why exactly I was pushing you away..." I laugh, shaking my head.

Bartlett's hungry eyes run over my body as the robe falls off my shoulder, exposing most of my breasts.

"I don't have to go anywhere," Bartlett tells me. "I'm right here, Abby. If you want to go back to the bedroom, I can turn off the kettle. Screw the tea and you can screw me instead."

This man really turns me on. His humor, his lack of pretense, the way he makes me feel like I don't have to look for the other shoe to drop. Even though I just met him, I feel like if I were going to fall, he'd catch me. Hijinx barks as he wanders into the kitchen. "I guess he woke up from his evening nap."

"You think he's hungry? We still have that bag of dog food from the hardware store."

We fill up a bowl for Hijinx, and after we let him out to go potty in the yard and bring him back inside, he snuggles up by the fireplace. Even though there isn't a fire blazing, he seems to realize that's the perfect place for a dog to sleep.

And with that, Bartlett takes my hand in his and leads me back to the bedroom.

This time I don't push him away; I don't let my insecurities about what might come next force me to miss out on what comes now. Because right now the bathrobe goes on the floor and his sweats are discarded.

What comes now is Bartlett running his hands all over my naked body as I begin to stroke his length up and down, up and down.

I kiss his chest, running my hand over his muscles, his ladder of abs. He is pure man. He is made out of God's green earth and being with him makes me feel alive in a way I haven't before. I know I haven't been a caged bird, but I felt trapped all my life.

I walked a tightrope and not just figuratively. I've been doing exactly as I was told for 21 years, performing not just for my parents but for everyone who came to our shows. None of it was because I asked for it. I was a product and I never wanted to be.

I want this. I want Bartlett. Now.

I give in to the moment as he lays me down on the bed, massaging my breasts until my nipples are hard and my pussy is wet.

He tells me I'm beautiful and I believe him because he is not a liar. He is a man of his word. He's one of those rare men who isn't trying. He just is.

"God, I love touching you," he tells me, his hot breath on my ear, his scruffy beard scratching my neck, making me feel deliriously happy and simply satisfied.

He's on top of me then, my legs wrapping around his body as his cock begins to enter me nice and slow.

"I don't want to hurt you," he whispers.

I close my eyes, gasping as he begins to fill me up slowly, inch by inch. It hurts. He's big and I'm tight, but I don't want this to stop. I don't want to *ever* stop feeling the way I feel right now.

Blissed out, beautiful, and meant to be.

"I don't want this night to end," I confess as we move as one, our fingers laced, his eyes locked on mine. My pussy drips and his cock fills me in a way I've never been filled before.

"Don't close your eyes; stay awake with me all night," he says. "We'll watch the sunrise."

"Don't you work tomorrow?" I ask with a gasp as he thrusts deeper into me, making me his in a whole new way.

"Sure I work tomorrow, but we're supposed to be here now, aren't we?"

"Right," I tell him. "We are. And the here and now? It's pretty damn perfect."

————

I WAKE UP IN A DAZE. Bartlett's arms wrapped around me tight, Hijinx in the center of the bed.

"I don't think I've slept that soundly in years," Bartlett tells me, stretching out in his king-size bed. He's bare-naked, and even though we said we weren't going to fall asleep, I think after we made love three times we both couldn't resist the temptation to cozy up in one another's arms and close our eyes.

And I'm glad now because the idea of a day without sleep was terrifying. I don't exactly want this man I just met to see me at my very worst.

We get ready for the day quickly – showers that lead to another round of sex – which, okay, I guess shower sex is just as fun as sex in his giant bed.

Then we're in his truck again, Hijinx on a leash at my feet. We park behind his hardware store in his designated spot in the alley.

"I'll walk you over to the police station," he says, "so you can get your wallet." Just then a flatbed truck comes through asking for Hammer Home's owner.

"That would be me," Bartlett says. "How can I help you?"

"I have a delivery, you able to take it now?" the man asks.

"Give me a sec." Bartlett turns to me. "You mind

hanging tight and we can go to the police station after I wrap this up?"

"I can get there, Bartlett. It's literally one block down Cozy Court, isn't it?"

Bartlett nods. "Yep, it's right next to the Home Cookin'. It's a diner across the street. Are you sure you're good?"

"Don't forget I have my guard dog." We both look down at Hijinx, who is sniffing the ground blindly.

I begin my walk down to the police department, taking in the town of Home early in the morning. Across the street, the owner of Home Made Bakery and Café is setting out tables and I can smell the coffee and espresso drinks.

Next to the bakery is Nested Home, the decor shop. There are flowers on display in the window along with beautiful candles and home decorations. It looks like the perfect place to buy a gift.

I cross Restful Road and pass the diner Bartlett mentioned. The booths are filled with plates of bacon and eggs and hash browns. Bartlett and I had oatmeal before we left his cabin so I'm not hungry, but I can imagine stopping there for a meal in the near future.

At the police department, I open the front doors and am greeted by a friendly officer at the front desk. Her badge says Darla. "How can I help you?" she asks.

"I'm looking for Officer Graham Rough? He has my wallet. He told me to stop in today to pick it up."

"Are you Abby? Oh, you poor thing." Darla stands, walking over to me. "I heard all about what happened yesterday. I cannot believe that is how you were welcomed to Home!"

"The day got better from there," I tell her. "I met the Rough family and they invited me to Sunday dinner, so that made up for it all."

Darla laughs. "Oh yeah? Dinner with the Roughs will do that. Annie and Red are sweethearts. Although the boys in that family are the biggest group of bachelors this town has ever met. Though the Rowdy boys over in Burly, well, they might even be less tameable than their cousins."

"There are more boys in that family?" I ask her.

"Yes, and they're all as handsome as the last." Darla smiles then walks back to her desk and grabs a key. "Graham isn't in until later this afternoon but I know where your wallet is. Let me grab it for you. I'll be right back."

A few minutes later I'm leaving the police station and headed toward the Home Run sports store, which apparently also serves as an electronics shop. I would never have thought that but Darla explained it to me.

I turn on Restful Road and take a right onto Snug Street and enter the sports store, with Hijinx on his leash.

"Hey," I ask the grey-haired man at the register. "I was wondering if you sell any phone chargers? I'm missing mine." I hand him my device.

"Sure thing," he says. "Though your phone is pretty old. I didn't even know people your age used flip phones anymore," he says with a laugh.

"Do you have a replacement charger?"

"Give me a minute. Let me look in a bin in the back."

I browse the sporting goods equipment and smile when I see the leotards and ballet slippers in one corner. It makes me wonder if there is a dance studio in town. I was never a dancer but am a gymnast at heart. I wasn't formally trained but I can do all sorts of tumbling and gymnastics. It's what I did under the big tent with my parents. I did more than tightrope walk, though that was my specialty.

The owner calls me over and tells me I'm in luck. "Found a charger, I have it plugged in right now. Want to leave it charging for a few minutes?"

"Yes, I feel lost without being able to listen to my messages."

He tells me his name is Harold and that I don't look familiar.

"I'm Abby and just came to Home yesterday on the train."

"Well, if you are looking for a car, my nephew Dale works at the mechanic shop in town, and you can tell him I sent you. He's an honest one."

"Good to know," I say. Harold tells me a little more about Home, and after twenty minutes of chitchat, my phone has 30% battery life.

"It's enough to get me going. And I think my dog needs to stretch his legs."

After I pay for the charger, he says, "Come again if you need any electronic or sporting good help."

"Actually, I was wondering if there is a dance or a gymnastics studio in town?"

"Nope, not since Miss Daisy moved to Seattle. Shame, isn't it? I still have all those leotards from when she used to teach dance."

I thank him again before heading outside. When I get into the cold winter air, I wrap my scarf around me again and kneel in front of Hijinx, offering him a doggie treat from my pocket. "Here you go, good boy," I tell him, giving him a kiss on his nose as he hungrily takes the dog treat.

Standing, I begin walking around the corner toward Tender Trail, where there is a bustling bike

and walking path that several people are out enjoy-
ing. Again, it is hard not to feel like a fish out of
water – like a girl who doesn't belong.

Everyone here is so damn perfect. I look down
at my scuffy boots and my worn blue jeans, tugging
on Hijinx's leash, leading him down the trail.
"Come on, boy." I open my phone as I walk,
pressing a button to listen to my voicemails.

The first one has me stopping in my tracks.

"Abby, we know where you're headed," my
father's voice slices through the winter day, sending
a chill through my body. "We're coming for you.
Don't think you can run away; we are your family."

I delete the message, listening to the next one.
"Abs, not sure why you think running from me is
an option," Ricky says. "I love you. You belong with
me. We're coming to get you. It won't be long now."

Panicked tears fill my eyes, and fear winds its
way through my belly.

Then someone comes up behind me, hand on
my shoulder.

I spin, shouting, "Don't touch me!"

7

BARTLETT

"ABBY," I say. "It's just me."

She's breathing fast. "Sorry," she says, wiping away the tears in her eyes. "I just, I got scared for a second there."

I shake my head, pulling her to me, wrapping my arms around her. "You don't have to apologize for anything." I kiss the side of her head protectively. Something shook her up, and she is probably traumatized after the guys attacked her yesterday. "Did you get your wallet?"

She nods, looking up into my eyes. "Yeah. Darla was at the police station. I guess Graham doesn't come in until later in the day."

I smile. "She's a nice lady, right?"

"Yeah, she seems to have lots to say about you

and your brothers, and your cousins, the Rowdy boys."

I take Abby's hand and walk down the sidewalk with her, Hijinx next to us on the leash. "Well, I think you'll figure it out pretty quickly that lots of people around here have opinions on the Roughs and Rowdys."

Abby shakes her head, looking up at me again. "I feel like you are this make-believe family. You're all way too good to be true."

"We're not as perfect as you might think. Every family has their skeletons, right?"

"You have skeletons in your closet?" Abby says. She rolls her eyes. "I don't believe it."

"Yeah? Well, my Great Grandpa Wilby Rough, he was born in 1910, bootlegged whiskey out of his barn here in Home with his wife, Margaret."

"That sounds like an urban legend," Abby says with a laugh.

"Apparently the cops shut him down because he was selling more liquor than anybody else on the west side of Washington."

Abby shakes her head. "I think this is a family story, not the real history of Home."

"Well, I guess we could always go to the Home History Museum and find out if it's truth or fiction."

Abby laughs. "There's a Home History Museum?"

"Of course there is. My Great-Great Grandpa Homer settled this town."

Abby groans. "Oh my God, you really are perfect, aren't you?"

"Stop it," I say, my hip hitting hers. "We're not using that word today, okay? I feel like there's too much pressure wrapped around it, and I don't want to spook you again like you got spooked last night."

Abby's fingers lace through mine a little bit tighter. "Yeah. Well, if I was spooked at first, I sure came around, didn't I?"

I chuckle. "Yeah, you certainly *came* around more than once."

"More than *twice*," she says with a laugh as we walk up to the Home Cookin'.

"You want some lunch?"

"It's a little early for lunch, isn't it?" Abby says.

I shrug. "I'm always hungry. I'm a big-ass mountain man."

"I guess you are, aren't you?" Abby smiles. "What should we do with Hijinx?"

"Maybe my sister, Lemon, could watch him a bit."

"Does she live around here?"

"Remember, she lives right next door to the bed and breakfast."

"Right," Abby says. "I think I'm still getting mixed up around town."

"Well, the town's not that big, but there are a lot of us Roughs. But let me give her a call real quick."

A few minutes later, after we've dropped Hijinx off at Lemon's so we can enjoy our lunch together, Abby and I settle into a booth at the only diner in town. Menus in hand, I ask her what she's having.

"Um, I think I'll take the grilled cheese and tomato soup," she tells our waitress, Cassidy.

"And what'll you have, Bartlett?" she asks.

"The usual," I tell her.

"Sounds good. Anything to drink?"

"Coffee," I say.

"Water's fine," Abby says. "Thank you."

Once Cassidy leaves, Abby smirks. "So they know your regular order here?"

I chuckle again. "I'm telling you, I was born and raised in this town. Yeah, Cassidy knows my order. I've known that girl since we were in grade school. Well, I was probably in junior high when she was in grade school. But yeah, same difference. Everyone around here has known each other forever."

"It's so crazy," Abby says. "I've never experienced anything like that."

"So your family was always on the road?" I ask her, wanting to get a better idea of what her family actually did on the road.

"Yeah," she says. She opens and closes the flip phone in her hand.

"Hey," I say, "you got your phone fixed?"

"Yeah," she says. "Harold at the sports store had a bin full of old chargers. That's all I needed."

"I'm surprised he had a charger that would work for a phone that looks like it's 10 years old," I say, teasing her.

"Hey," she says, "if it ain't broke, why fix it?"

"Fair enough," I say. "So he had a charger that works and you're good to go?"

Abby nods. "Yep. Good as new. So now I'll have to get your phone number and put it in my phone."

"That old flip phone can hold contacts?"

Abby rolls her eyes. "And now you're messing with me. Yes, I can even text on this thing," she says. Just then, her phone buzzes. She opens it and she reads whatever message has come through. Her eyes darken as she reads the screen, and she quickly closes it and shoves it in her coat pocket.

"Anything important?" I ask.

She shakes her head. "Nothing important."

"Is it your family looking for you?"

"Something like that," Abby says dismissively. "So, winter in Home is pretty cold," she says. "My cheeks were freezing the entire time I was walking Hijinx on the trail. You ever feel like you're freezing your butt off out here in the mountains?"

I laugh, but I'm still pretty aware that she's been changing the subject every time I try to talk about where she's come from, where she's headed. As much as I'm falling for this girl, I know Rye's right. I don't know much about her and I need to if I want to see this going anywhere. "So what are your plans, Abby? I mean, I know you said you came through here when you were younger and you always wanted to come back when you got a chance, but are you planning on settling down in Home?"

Her eyes meet mine as Cassidy brings us our lunch, my BLT and French fries, her grilled cheese and soup. "Thanks Cassidy," I say as she walks away.

"I think I could see myself here," Abby says apprehensively, picking up half of her sandwich and dipping it in the red soup. "I'd like to believe I could stay here. I need a job, and I need a place to live. Harold said I could talk to his son, Dale, about getting a car."

I nod, listening, wanting to believe she wants to settle down here. But I've known her a day. I don't want to get spun up in someone that might not be here tomorrow.

"What?" she asks. "You don't think I'm sticking around material?"

She's literally read my mind. I frown. "I didn't say that."

"I know you didn't say that," she presses, "but it's what you're thinking. I mean, you're Bartlett Rough. It's like Darla said at the station. You're pretty much the epitome of the perfect package. Even Cassidy's looking at you like she wants you."

"Cassidy is nothing to me," I say. "I mean it. We never went to school together, and she's a lot younger than me. We never–"

"Regardless," Abby says, cutting me off, "you and me, I don't know, Bart. It seems like a fantasy."

"Are you always like this?" he asks me. "Pushing away the good things before you've truly gotten a chance to experience them?"

She takes another bite of her sandwich, ignoring my question or maybe thinking it through. "Bartlett, I'm just scared. Scared of a place as perfect as Home."

After lunch, I head back to the hardware store and Abby goes over to Lemon's to pick up Hijinx. While I'm in the shop, Rye comes in.

"Abby around?" he asks.

I shake my head. "No, she's over at Lemon's. Why? You have something to say to her?"

He shrugs, his knuckles rapping on the counter. "Actually, I have something to say to you first. Look, you're not going to like this."

"What is it?" I ask, my patience already thin.

"Well, you know my buddy, Walker? He works over at the train station."

"Course I know Walker. We went to school with him, right?"

"Yeah. Well, he owed me a favor and he looked at the manifestos from yesterday's trains. There was no one with the name Abby on any of the trains."

"Well, maybe she didn't have a ticket."

"She's just catching trains up from California or wherever she comes from without a ticket? That's not how trains work anymore. This isn't 1943," Rye says with a snort. "Come on, think. You know who she is?"

"What? You think she's a liar? Fuck you, Rye. You think you know everything?"

"No. I just know Walker, who happens to run the train station, and I'm telling you, something's up."

"Look, I'm not interested in your fucking inter- ference, okay?"

Just then, the bells on the front door ring and Abby comes in with Hijinx, who begins to bark at my older brother. I can't help but smile at that. Even the dog knows Rye is bad news.

"This is ridiculous," Rye says. "You're going to get yourself in some real trouble, you know that?"

Rye walks away, pushing open the hardware store door without a word.

Abby watches him go before coming over to me. "So what's that about?"

But right then, several customers enter the store asking for help. "Look, I can't talk right now," I say, turning to her. "I'm sorry, but I've got to help my customers. But I'll come find you when my employee, Luke, comes in. He'll be here in a half an hour."

"That's fine," Abby says. "We can meet up later. I'm going to take Hijinx to the park."

"Will you be warm enough?" I ask. "I have some hand warmers on aisle four."

She smiles at that, kissing my cheek. "I'll be fine," Abby says, reaching for the gloves in her coat pocket. "Look, just take care of yourself and whatever's going on with your brother. We can meet up later, all right?"

I nod, watching her go before returning to my customers, who are looking for salt for their icy driveway, shovels for their yards. I need to do my job, but still I can't shake my annoyance at my brother.

Rye sends me a text with screenshots of various train manifestos, but I don't want to even look at them, I'm so pissed at him. I've been doing what everybody wants for me for years. Rye thinks he knows everything because he's my big brother.

Well, fuck that. I know myself and I care about Abby. When I'm with her, I feel something real. So why not take a chance on that?

Why not take a chance on her?

8

ABBY

LEAVING THE HARDWARE STORE, it's hard to not let my insecurities flare up. I know Rye doesn't like me. I heard as much last night when I was at his parents' house. I'm not sure what he was telling Bartlett just now, but it wasn't good. The moment I walked into the hardware store, he walked out.

Right next door to Hammer Home is the Mystic Shop and I pause, looking in the store windows. The display is beautiful. It's full of crystals and tarot card decks. There are luscious ferns and beautiful velvet curtains.

"What do you think, Hijinx?" I ask, tugging on my dog's leash. Though he can't see anything, I wonder if he can sense the aura changing here, the energy. It's sure a lot better than the energy Rye left behind when he saw me and stormed out.

I twist my lips, wondering if I should go into the crystal shop and see if there's a palm reader in there. When I was with my parents in the circus, there were a few fortune tellers over the years. One of them in particular, Lucinda, would always take my palm in hers and trace the lines down the center of it, telling me I would live a long and happy life. I think she told most people that, because no one wanted to hear a tragic story when they were out for a little bit of fun.

I always wondered what she would tell me if she were really going to give it to me straight. If she'd tell me my life was always going to be hard. Because it's felt like that. It's felt like it's always been a struggle. My parents have always looked at me like I am their golden ticket. The final act in their show. Never like I am their daughter, someone they care about.

I keep walking down the street. I cross Warm Way and I see the edge of the Rough River. Sitting on a park bench, I cross my legs and take in the view. I can see my breath. It's so cold out, but I have gloves on and I pull Hijinx up on the bench next to me. He rests his head in my lap and I pet him, taking a deep breath in, letting it out slow.

He has always been my center. For years. Last night at Red and Annie's house, it was hard to imagine what it would be like to really be in a family like that. Growing up around a table where there was always another seat pulled out, welcoming a stranger in.

My parents were always so secretive. So on edge. It was always about keeping people away. Shielding the dark corners of our circus tent. My dad's drinking. My mom's affairs. Me, cast aside.

I'm lost in these thoughts when Bartlett sits down next to me, two paper cups in hand.

"I thought you might like some coffee to warm you up."

I smile, taking the paper cup from his hand. "Thanks," I say.

"I wasn't sure what you liked. I know it's not Christmas anymore, but I was hoping you might like a peppermint mocha."

I smile. "Who doesn't like a peppermint mocha?"

He grins and takes a drink of his.

"Thank you," I say.

"Of course," he says. He leans back on the bench, his arm wrapping around my shoulders like we've done this dozens, hundreds of times, not like this is the first. The first time we've sat on a bench looking out at the river together.

"So you were thinking something pretty heavy. I could tell," he says, and his voice is deep and clear. Just like that river. And I wonder how a man like him, whom I've just met, can see straight through me so damn well.

"How could you tell?" I ask.

He gives me a half smile that rends my heart in two. "You looked sad out here. I was wondering if maybe you heard more of what Rye was saying than I thought."

"I know your brother doesn't like me," I say, twisting my lips.

"I'm sorry. Rye doesn't really like anybody."

I nod. "I gathered that. He's a little bit of a grump, huh?"

"He's been alone too long."

"He's never been in love?"

"Not once."

"Not even with Plum?" I say. "Surely that girl could even melt the burliest mountain man's heart."

Bartlett laughs. "She was my first love, that's for sure."

"Your first?" I ask. We haven't gone deep enough to touch on his past relationships. "And your second?"

Bartlett's eyes reach mine. He swallows. "I feel like I'm falling for you," he says, "in the space of a day. Rye would probably call me crazy, but I think there are crazier things than knowing what you want and giving someone a chance."

My heart pounds at his vulnerability. "I don't deserve that," I say.

"Deserve what?" he counters.

"The truth."

"Everyone deserves the truth."

I bite my bottom lip. "Do you want to talk about why Rye was so mad?"

"Not really," Bartlett says, "but I will." He runs a hand over his jaw, takes another drink of his peppermint mocha. "He says you weren't on the train manifesto." Bartlett shakes his head. "He has a buddy who works at the train station. He was able to get the records, I guess, of everyone who came through on the trains the last few days and there was no Abby. I told him that maybe you had hopped the train, you know? That Jack Kerouac shit we talked about. Maybe you didn't have a ticket. Maybe–"

I take his hand. "That's not why I wasn't on the manifesto," I say, shaking my head, exhaling. "My name isn't Abby."

"It's not?" he says, looking at me like I'm a stranger.

"No, it's not. It's–" I groan, dropping my head back. "My name is a lot worse than Abby. It's Abracadabra."

"What?" Bartlett looks at me like I'm literally crazy.

"Don't laugh," I say. "I mean I–"

"Did you say your name's *Abracadabra*?"

"Hey, your mom named you after food. I don't think you get to judge me." I groan again. "Oh my God. This is mortifying, but my family... We're in the circus. We *are* the circus. That's why I've been here before. Remember, you told me the story about when you were a little kid, how you remember the year the circus came to town. Well, that was my family. We're a traveling circus show. And my parents thought they were so clever when they named me, their only child, Abracadabra. I've only ever gone by Abby. But my license," I pull it out of my coat pocket, showing him my ID, "look, Abracadabra. Officially, yep, that's me." I hold the picture next to my face, grinning like a dork.

Bartlett cracks up. Like actually cracks up. Knee slapping, belly laughing. "Oh my God," he said. "I never could have imagined that." He pulls out his phone and begins scrolling through texts. "You are Abracadabra," he says. "Fucking Rye. That guy thinks he's such a fucking know-it-all. I told him I didn't care what the manifesto said or what he thought."

"Really?" I say. "You told him you didn't care what he discovered? This horrifying truth about me, the liar." I blink at the realization that Bartlett stood up for me. He believed in me.

"Yeah," he says, taking my hand. "I feel something here. Real. Something really real with you, Abby– I mean, Abracadabra."

"I always hated my name," I say, pressing a finger to his lip. "But somehow when you say it, it doesn't sound so bad. But still, it's not something I go spreading around."

"I think it's cute," he says, giving me a kiss. Then he grins again. "It was on the papers," he says, "and your driver's license. I don't think it's quite as secret as you think."

"I never tell anyone my real name," I admit. "But now you know."

"Yes," he says. He shows me the phone. "Look," he tells me, "your name is right here. You came in on the train yesterday at 2:30."

"Yes, I did," I say. "Ever since I was here when I was a little girl, I've wanted to come back. I was only here for a few nights with my family doing that show, but I thought this town was magic. And now I feel like it's magic in a whole new way."

"Why is that?" Bartlett asks, cupping my cheek, tucking a strand of my hair behind my ear and looking at me like I am precious.

"After meeting your family and seeing how much they care about you, how much they want you to be happy – even Rye, his intentions were good – it just reminds me that my family, they don't care about my happiness at all." I tell him about my parents. How I'd asked to leave the traveling show for years and they wouldn't let me. "I had to save up money behind their backs so I could go. They want me to marry this guy, Ricky. He was one of the performers in the show. They love him. And for all the wrong reasons. Mostly because he's my dad's drinking buddy. And I knew if I stayed any longer, I'd end up with him. And I couldn't let that happen."

"That's why you ran."

"Yeah. That's why I ran. They've been calling me," I say. "I got these voice messages this morning, after I got my phone charged, and," tears fill my eyes, "I hate it, Bartlett. It's hard to not be bitter, you know? I just want to be happy. That's why I came here. Because I'm just aching for a fresh start. I thought maybe if I came Home, maybe I'd get one. But I'm scared that they're going to find me and take that happiness away."

Bartlett wraps me in his arms, holding me tight. "As long as I've got you, no one is going to take you anywhere."

9

BARTLETT

I GET Abby in my truck, Hijinx in her lap, and I crank up the heat. "Okay," I say, looking at her as I pull out of town, headed toward my cabin. "Here's the plan. We're going to get back to the cabin, rest and change, and then I'm going to take you out on the town."

She laughs. "Okay. I like the beginning of that, but you don't have to take me out, Bartlett. Don't you have to go back to work or something?"

I shake my head, running my hand over her thigh, hating that her jeans are getting in the way between my hand and her bare skin. "No, my guys are closing up tonight. I'm thinking a nice dinner, candlelight. What do you say?"

"They have a fancy restaurant in Home?" Abby

asks with a smirk. "I haven't seen anything like that."

"Well, you don't know everything that there is here. And, in fact, there's a popup restaurant tonight called Home Grown. It's this bougie place with all organic vegetables, farm-raised beef, and nice wine from organic farms."

"Ooh," Abby says, shrugging her shoulders. "Sounds fancy."

"And I already got us a reservation. Well, Lemon got us a reservation."

"Really?" Abby says. "You did that, even though you thought I was this lying girl who didn't even come in on a train?"

"I knew you came in on a train, and I never thought you were a liar. That was Rye, and he was wrong, Abracadabra."

Abby laughs. "Oh, my God. I can't believe you found out my real name."

"I'm going to find everything out about you sooner or later," I say. "I mean, if you'll let me."

Abby licks her lips. Now it's her turn to run her hand up and down my thigh, over my thick cock that's growing harder by the minute.

"Oh, I'm interested in learning all kinds of things about one another," she says. "Last night we didn't learn quite enough, did we?"

"Not even close," I growl as I pull up to my

cabin, putting my truck in park and practically dragging that woman inside.

Hijinx is passed out by the fire soon enough, and her and me? We're stripping our clothes in the bathroom. Our jeans are on the floor. The hot water is cranked up high. Her panties are at her ankles, and her bra is lost. Just like me. I'm lost in her body, her eyes, her tits, her ass. Fuck, this girl is incredible.

"What?" she asks as I shake my head, looking her over, up and down, and loving every damn inch.

"I really like the way you look," I tell her. "And I like the way you laugh, and the way you think, and the way you are."

"That's a lot of compliments for a girl who has spent her life thinking she wasn't quite enough."

"I don't even know what you did in the circus," I say. "Tell me everything. Were you a contortionist? Fuck, please tell me you were a contortionist."

She laughs, hard. "Oh, my God, you are such a man."

I stroke my cock up and down, and then I take her hand, showing her where she belongs. She begins to take hold of me the way I need her to as we step into the shower. I turn on the second shower head and then, fuck, it's bliss. Her and me, there. Wet, aching, ready.

"I was not a contortionist," she says, the water running in rivulets over her breasts, her hair. She looks so sexy and my body is primed to take her. My cock is aching for her sweet, tight pussy. But first, I want to enjoy this moment, this steamy shower made for two.

"I was a tightrope walker," she says, her eyes widening. "What do you think of that?"

"You can balance then, huh?"

She nods. "Yeah."

"You think you can balance on my cock?"

She laughs; her head falls back. "Oh, my God. Yeah, I think I can."

"Good," I say. I lift her up and I place her back against the tiled wall of the shower, lowering her down on my thick cock.

"Oh, yes," she moans as she sinks down on me.

"There you go, baby. Just like that."

"Oh, fuck," she moans loudly.

"Just nice and slow," I tell her, but there's no such thing. My cock is hungry. Her pussy is willing and, fuck, it's time to take her for a ride. She begins to bounce. Those tits of hers are squeezed against my chest and I kiss her mouth hard.

Her tongue finds mine and I inhale that woman. I take her like I've never taken her before. I fuck her against the shower wall as she rides me up and down, bouncing like a little toy. My toy.

"Yeah. I guess you can balance, can't you?" I say, pulling back from the kiss and looking into her eyes. My hand on her ass, she wraps her arms around my neck, holding on for her fucking life.

"Oh, my God," she whimpers as I fuck her nice and good the way she deserves and needs and didn't even know was fucking possible.

"Is this what you've been waiting for?" I ask her. "Is this what you were hoping was going to happen when you came Home?"

"This is better than I imagined," she says, panting in my ear, sucking on my earlobe, as I begin to thrust deeper into her tight channel. She cries out as she comes, her sweet slit dripping as I finish.

I lift her up and off of me, her toes touching the tiled floor, and she spins around, her hands on the wall, her cheek against the cool tile. My hands running up and down the curve of her back, between her legs, over her pussy. My fingers diving deep into her sweet hole, finger-fucking her. Catching her off guard as I do.

"Oh, God," she cries, gripping the wall for something, anything, to hold onto as she grinds her ass against my hand. I begin to finger her harder, my cock growing by the second, and she loves it. "I need you." She's ready for more. Hungry, willing, able.

"Me too, baby. Me too." I get her cunt nice and ripe, and then, before she knows what's happening, she begins to tense around my fingers, coming all over again against my hand. She cries out, louder this time, and it's hot as hell.

When she finishes, she spins around, looking up at me with eyes filled with wonder, lust, and something deeper, something more.

"Oh, my God," she says. "You're making me..."

"What?" I say. "Tell me."

"You're making me want to stay forever."

"Good," I say. "Then I better keep fucking you so you never leave."

She drops to her knees and begins to stroke my cock up and down. The water from the shower head is still nice and warm, and she begins to suck my cock like my fucking queen. I look at her on her knees, pleasuring me, and my cock hardens, aching under her suction.

"Oh, God," I groan, looking at her perfection, her mouth nice and tight. Those lips sucking me, her head bobbing up and down as she gets me off like a good lover. My lover.

I'm not letting this girl go. Ever. My cock is hungry and ready, and my hot seed shoots out from my tip, filling her mouth. I watch as she swallows, filling her belly. "Fuck," I groan, gripping the wall as I finish.

She keeps sucking, up and down, her hands playing with my balls. They're tight, tense, until I'm done. She stands. She smiles. She licks her lips.

"I've never done that before," she says. "How'd I do?"

"Don't ask a question like that," I say. "You know how you did."

She grins. "That good, huh?"

I nod, drawing her mouth to mine. "Fuck, Abby. Forget the past. We are the perfect fucking pair."

10

ABBY

I DON'T HAVE anything to wear to a candlelit dinner, so Bartlett makes a call to his sister. I'm expecting Lemon to show up with clothes for me, but, surprisingly, it's Fig who stops by an hour later.

"Hey. Sorry I didn't get much of a chance to talk to you last night," she says with a shrug. She takes off a big, furry pink coat and a matching faux fur hat. "I know I was being a little melodramatic, but, you know, that's just me," she says, scrunching up her face. "Hey, Bart, Mom said to bring you this." She hands him a bag and he opens it immediately.

"Mm," he says. "Mom must have been in a good mood today, huh?"

Fig laughs. "Yes, because after I realized I was being a brat at dinner, I told her I was finished with the idea of studying abroad for the end of my senior year and that I would drop the whole thing."

"So, she went on a baking spree today?" Bartlett asks.

"What did she make?" I ask, curious about the family dynamics.

Fig's eyes brighten. "She made her almond thumbprint cookies and her famous vanilla bean scones. You'll love them. They were my Uncle Luke's favorites."

"Were?" I ask, not sure how personal is too personal but also wanting to know everything about this family.

Fig and Bart share a kind look. Bartlett clears his throat. "He was my dad's best friend. We lost him last year; he died in a car accident up on Rickshaw Ridge. It's a bad bend up in the woods."

Fig smiles softly, a hand on her brother's arm. "Well, when you have those scones with your morning coffee, remember to tell Abby some of those tall tales he always wowed us with when we were little. I mean, if you're staying here?" She winks at me. "Okay. I *know* you're staying here. Everyone in town knows you're staying here. I heard what happened with Mary last night."

"How did you hear what happened with Mary last night?" I ask.

Fig smirks. "Mary told Mom. Mom told me."

I'm on the couch and there's a fire blazing. We don't have reservations for this popup restaurant for another 90 minutes, and I have on cozy clothes while I'm waiting for my hair to air dry.

Fig, on the other hand, looks like she's just stepped out of a fashion magazine, which is surprising considering she lives in a small town. But she has on heeled boots, patchwork denim jeans, an oversized sweater with a blouse under it, jewelry, and a full face of makeup. Somehow, though, she looks effortless, like she could be an Instagram influencer.

Me, I don't have a stitch of anything on my face, or my hair, or my nails. I am as salt-of-the-earth as they come.

I take in Fig's big, bold personality as she plops down on the couch with a large tote bag under her arm that I'm just now noticing. "So, why did you give up on your dream of being a foreign exchange student for your last few months of high school?" I ask her, knowing it's a bit of a pry.

"Because Mom promised me that I could go on a trip for spring break."

"One trip is better than a whole semester in Europe?" Bartlett asks. "Doesn't seem like much of a compromise."

Fig shrugs. "Well, I realized Mom and Dad are never going to actually let me go. So, I was probably being a little bit of a baby with my whole, you know, tantrum."

I smile. Fig may be dramatic, but at least she has some understanding of the family dynamic and the way she comes off. "So, where are you going on your trip?"

She smiles. "I don't know yet. What do you think I should do? Have you ever gone anywhere cool?"

"I've gone to some cool places. I've spent a lot of time in California," I tell her. "Santa Monica's awesome, and Santa Cruz is really cool. They both have great beaches. Have you ever been surfing?"

"Never," she says. "I've hardly been to the ocean at all. The only beaches I've been to are the ones here in Washington and in Oregon, which are, like, totally frigid."

I laugh. "You've never been to a warm beach, like in Florida?"

"Never," she says. "You have?"

"Yeah. My family has traveled around a lot."

"Lucky," she says.

I shrug. "It's all relative, I suppose, huh?"

Bartlett meets my eyes, and I know what he's thinking, that it really is all so relative. What I wouldn't have traded to have a life like Fig's. "Well, I guess you have some time to think about it. Spring break is, what, March or April?"

"April. And it's only January now. So, I suppose you're right."

"Who will you go on your trip with?" Bart asks. "Don't tell me you have some boyfriend now."

"As if Mom and Dad would let me go on a trip with a boy. No. I'm going to go with Mom." Fig smiles. "And Lemon. Unless, you know, something crazy happens and Lemon's married by then."

Bart snorts. "Yeah, right. That girl is more frigid than a Washington beach. I don't think she'll ever get married."

"Geez," Fig says. "You never know. Someone might come into town and sweep your little sister off her feet."

"Are you talking about you or Lemon?" I tease.

Fig smiles. "I'm never getting married," she says. "I'm going to be single forever. Living in Paris, smoking cigarettes, and sipping on gin. It's going to be glorious."

"And what are you going to do in Europe?" I ask.

"I'm going to be a fashion designer," she says with a flourish. "Speaking of, I have the most amazing outfits for you." She opens her bag and begins holding up different dresses for me to choose from. "I didn't know if you were a velvet kind of girl, or more of a silk girl, but I mean, with your body, you could really wear anything. Speaking of, what kind of work do you do?"

"I'm a gymnast," I tell her as simply as possible.

"Really?" Her eyes widen, impressed. "That's, like, a real job?"

"Yeah," I snort. "It's a real job. I can do all sorts of stunts."

"Wow, that's amazing. Can you show me something?"

"Uh, sure," I say, and then I look around Bartlett's room, noticing the rail across the loft. I walk up the flight of stairs and climb up to the railing.

"Stop," Bartlett cries. "Don't get up there. You'd be twenty feet in the air!"

"I'm fine," I laugh.

Fig shakes her head. "What are you doing, Abby? You're going to kill yourself."

"Sorry," I grimace. "I told you I was a gymnast."

Fig has shock written on her face. "My God. You're going to break your neck."

I shrug. And, instead of climbing on top of the railing, I walk back down the stairs. "Fine," I say. "I won't show you my tricks."

Fig doesn't think I am being serious and just laughs. "Okay. You're super crazy. Also, you're perfect for Bart because he is so straight and narrow, he needs a crazy girl like you."

I scrunch up my nose, thinking she has no idea. She thinks her brother is all wound up tight, but a little bit ago, when he was in the shower with me, he was nice and easy.

I lick my lips, thinking if Bartlett was going to see me in a dress, he'd probably prefer me in something tight. "I'd say silk," I tell her, pointing to the tiniest dress out of the options.

Fig nods. "It's going to look stunning on you. And I have tights and heels, and a little fur coat. Come on," she says, scooching me down the hall. "It's time for you to get dressed."

Thirty minutes later, Fig has me decked out in the most glamorous look I've ever had on. She's even curled my hair a bit, and my eyelashes, and added some mascara for good measure. "I don't think your brother's going to recognize me," I tell her.

She smiles. "He's going to love it," she says. "Besides, Bartlett needs a reason to have a little sparkle in his life."

"Why do you say that?" I ask.

"I don't know. He's always been the good guy, done the right thing. Maybe it's just time for him to have some fun."

"I'm more than fun," I say.

"I know," Fig says, "but you can be good and fun, and I think maybe he needs both."

"So, you approve? Because Rye doesn't."

"Oh, Rye doesn't know anything," she says. "He's a big bossy boy who knows nothing about the real world."

I fight back a smile. The baby of the family might be the smartest one of all. "Thank you for helping me," I tell her. "I'm an only child, so I don't know what it's like to get ready with sisters and have siblings drop by, but I appreciate it."

She grins. "Well, my sister is super bossy, and most of my brothers are too. So I appreciate having a *nice* girl around for a change," she says haughtily, giving me a wink and blowing me a kiss.

When Bartlett sees me, he lets out a low whistle that tells me everything I need to know. He takes my hand and gives me a kiss and makes sure I feel like I'm the most beautiful girl in the world. Hijinx is happy and asleep in the cabin, and Bartlett drives me into town.

Home Grown is a popup restaurant tucked next to the toy store. And, apparently, the space rotates into different establishments throughout the year. Everyone knows Bartlett when we enter, and they look me over, but they all give me warm smiles.

"I feel like they're staring," I say.

Bartlett whispers in my ear, his breath hot, warm, burning me up. "Of course, they're staring," he says. "You are the most beautiful woman in this place."

At the table with candlelight between us, he orders wine that is expensive and delicious, and we get steaks and mashed potatoes and green beans, and we eat until our hearts are content and our bellies are full and our eyes are glazed over with lust and desire and memories of the last 48 hours.

"I don't know what's happening," I murmur. "I think there's a spell on this town and it's been spun on me too."

"Is that a good thing?" he asks.

"It's a great thing," I say.

After dinner, he leads me down Snug Street and stops right in front of the Home History Museum.

"I got the keys," he said.

"What for?" I ask.

"Well, I thought I might tell you a little bit more about Home."

I smile as he opens the door and lets us inside.

"I told you. My ancestors started this town in 1910. They settled here, Homer and Annabel Rough, after they got married in 1909 in Seattle. They moved up here, found this mountain, and settled this land."

I smile, listening to him as we wander the museum. It's dark and romantic and quiet, and the night feels like ours in a way a night never has before. There are pictures on the walls that tell a story, that tell *his* story, and I feel like I'm going back in time. I hear about Welby Rough, who married Margaret.

"He's the one who was making the whiskey in his barn?"

"Legend has it," Bartlett laughs. "And he had a sister named Annie and another named Lucy. Though, Lucy disappeared in Oregon around 1935."

"You remember all this?"

He laughs. "Hey, I'm a family man. You should know that. Do you want kids?"

I nod. "I do," I say. "Do you?"

He laughs. "Yeah. Though, I wasn't thinking of seven."

"Me either," I say, "but a few."

"Same," he says with a smile. His hands are on mine, my heart bubbling up with want, with hope, as he continues to recite his family tree. "That's my grandfather, Reynold Rough, who married Rosie. They had Redford and Filson, brothers, who then each married a wife of their own. Red married Annie, and became my mom and dad, and Filson married Ruby."

"And where do your aunt and uncle live?" I ask him.

"Oh, they live on the mountain."

"They have any kids?" I ask.

"Yeah. Wyatt and Willa. They're a few years older than us, but neither of them are married."

"Interesting," I say. "And how did your parents meet?" I ask him.

He grins. "Now, that's a story for another day, and you'd have to ask them because my mom gets mad if any of us kids get it wrong."

"Okay," I say. "I can honor that. And if your whole family settled here, and if this whole family tree is your family history, what happens next for you?" I ask. "Does the line just continue?"

"Yeah," he says. His eyes find mine. "With the right woman, the family tree grows more branches, Abby."

I swallow, feeling scared because I realize this – him – it's all I want.

He must sense something stirring within me because he wraps me up in his arms, and he holds me tight. There isn't any music playing, but we slow dance in that museum, imagining a life that has roots going deep in the town of Home.

11

BARTLETT

A WEEK with Abby and my life has changed.

She makes me feel like anything is possible. And that may sound corny, but only if you've never been in love.

"Love?" Lemon says, shaking her head at me. She's brought in muffins from Home Made, the bakery across the street, and hands me a blueberry one. "You can't be in love with someone after knowing them for a week. That's ridiculous."

I shrug. "When you know, you know."

"Have you told her this?" she asks me with a frown, eyes narrowed.

"Not yet, but I plan on telling her after family dinner this Sunday."

Lemon groans. "That's so romantic. Let me

guess. You're going to take her out behind the house, up to the old treehouse, and point out a star, and–"

"Hey," I say. "That was my plan."

"Oh, my God," Lemon says. "You are such a boy."

"I was trying to be romantic," I say.

She laughs. "Well, I think it's ridiculous."

"I just think you're jaded. Why aren't you more optimistic?" I ask. "If memory serves me correctly, your best friend, Juniper, met her husband, Jacob, in the most random way in Alaska not even two months ago."

Lemon takes a giant bite of her muffin to avoid answering my question. I laugh. "Exactly," I say. "When they came home for Christmas, I don't think I've ever seen two people more in love in my life. They were all heart eyes and lovey-dovey. It was cute. And Juniper deserves to be happy. That girl has had a hard life and Jacob makes her happy."

"True," Lemon says. "I am happy for Juniper and Jacob, and they are happy together. Happy, happy, happy." She groans. "But that's one in a million. What are the chances of you falling in love equally as fast just one month later? Not statistically possible."

"You're not even good at math, woman," I tease as Plum comes into the store with her dad, Rueben.

"Hey," Rueben says with a smile. "What are you joking about?"

"Oh, I'm just giving our big brother here a hard time," Lemon says, wrapping her arms around Plum. "He thinks he's in love."

"With Abracadabra," Plum says with a grin.

"Abraca-what?" Lemon asks.

I press a finger to my lip. "Shh," I say. "That was our secret, Plum."

Plum giggles. "Sorry, Uncle Bart. But I have big news," she says.

"What's the news?" Lemon asks.

"The circus is coming to town," Plum says, jumping up and down. "Look." She shows us a flyer and sure enough the Big Top Circus is coming to town this weekend. Today is Thursday.

My stomach drops.

"What kind of circus performs in the middle of winter?" Rueben asks. "Kind of weird, right?"

This is more than weird. This is downright messy.

"Well," Lemon says, looking at the flyer more closely, "they're setting up at the Burly Fairgrounds. That's under cover and heated. That makes more sense. Are you guys going to go tomorrow?" she asks Rueben.

"Please, Daddy. Please, please, please," Plum asks, jumping up and down as Abby comes into the store.

She's smiling, having no idea that her whole world is about to come to a halt. "Hey guys," she says. I walk right over to her and give my girl a kiss. Damn, I like that. My whole world has expanded with her in it. My eyes? They're hearts too. Juniper and Jacob, Lemon's friends, aren't the only ones who are head over heels.

"So, I've got great news," she says. "I heard that Home Brew is hiring. And I think that they might call me later for an interview. So, fingers crossed." She's been looking for a job the last few days. And while we haven't said anything about where she's going to be living because, well, I want her to live with me, nowhere else, we are talking about employment, which seems like a safer subject.

"That's awesome," I say. "Of course they'll hire you. They'd be lucky to have you."

Lemon nods. "Yeah. And I'm totally tight with the owner. Griffin and I were in 4-H together for years. I can totally give her a good word if you want."

"Of course," Abby says. "That's super nice."

"Abby," Plum says, jumping up and down and reaching for her hand. "Did you hear the other good news?"

"What's that?" Abby asks.

"The circus is coming to town tomorrow," she says. "Look." She hands Abby the flyer. "Dad says he's going to take me. Do you want to come? Daddy, can Abby come with us?"

Abby takes a flyer from Plum's hand and she takes a step back. Her face goes completely white as she takes in the news. "Oh God. Oh God," she says. "This is bad."

"Bad," Lemon says. "What's going on?"

"It's my family. This is my family's circus."

Rueben frowns. My family is a big family. So even though I filled my parents in on the situation with Abby and her parents, not all my siblings know because there's a lot of us and it's a complicated story. And like Lemon has explained over and over again, it's only been a week.

"Well, if it's your family, that's a good thing, right?" Lemon says. "Maybe they could come over to Mom and Dad's on Sunday for family dinner and–"

"No," Abby says, cutting Lemon off. "They're not coming to your parents' house ever," she says. "You don't understand. This is terrible. This is like..."

Plum begins to cry, looking up at her dad. "Daddy, why is the circus bad?"

Rueben picks Plum up. "It's nothing, honey."

"I'm sorry," Abby says. "Plum, the circus is fine. I

didn't mean to scare you. I just, I used to work in that circus," she says, blinking back her tears. "And it's just not the best place." She shakes her head, feeling trapped, stuck. I see it.

"You don't have to explain everything right now," I say. "What we actually need to do is call Graham down at the station."

Rueben's eyes widen as he takes in the seriousness of the situation. "Hey, Lemon," he says, "why don't you take Plum home? I'll come get her in a little while."

"Of course," Lemon says, realizing what's going on. "We're just going to go upstairs for a minute and grab a few things. I have my purse and my jacket up there."

"Actually," I say, "Abby, why don't you go with them, all right?" I give her a kiss on the cheek. "Rueben and I, we're going to go talk to Graham and we'll be right back, okay?"

"Are you sure?"

"Yes," I say. "I'm sure. All right?" I give her another kiss and then I watch her and my sister and Plum go upstairs to the office that is above the hardware store.

Rueben looks at me. "What in the hell is going on?" he asks.

I run a hand over my beard. "Her parents

trapped her, kept her basically a prisoner for years. And if they're coming back into town, they're coming for one thing and one thing only."

Rueben nods, understanding. "They're coming for her."

12

ABBY

ONCE LEMON GRABS her coat and purse from upstairs, we head back outside to her cottage down the street. Plum is confused by what's going on, but Lemon's a good aunt and explains to her that there is nothing to worry about. "Your dad and uncle just had to go run an errand," she says, looking at me and whispering over Plum's head. "Are you okay?"

I nod, because I am. Bartlett has texted telling me that he's at the police station and talking to his brother Graham. Apparently, they're all on it. They saw some semis with the Big Top Circus logo come through on the way to Burly already, headed to the fairgrounds.

He tells me he'll meet up with me soon and that everything is going to be fine. Wanting to believe him, I put my doubt behind me and head over to Lemon's place.

Just as we get to her house, though, I get a phone call from a number I don't recognize. Thinking it might be my father calling me from an unknown number, giving me information and insight on his plans, I take the call.

"Hello," I say, apprehensive at best.

"Hey, is this Abby?" a woman's warm voice asks.

"This is her."

"My name's Griffin. I'm the manager over at Home Brew. I heard you were looking for a job and we are in desperate need of a hostess. Do you think you might be able to come over now and we could have a little chat? I know it's short notice, but I'm hoping to hire someone for next week. So if we could talk now..." I smile, my shoulders instantly dropping. "That's awesome," I say. "And yeah, I'm free right now. I can be over there in just a few minutes."

"Perfect," she says. "I'll be expecting you."

I end the phone call and fill Lemon and Plum in.

"Why don't we walk over there together," Lemon says. "I'd feel better about that. I think Bartlett would be mad if I let you out of my sight."

I smile, appreciating her concern. And

together the three of us walk down Delightful Drive.

Home Brew is a bustling restaurant and bar, and I can imagine working here the moment I step inside the rustic space. The interview goes great. And Griffin is as nice as Lemon told me. She offers me the job if I want it, which I do.

"Perfect," she says. "So, if you can start on Monday, that would be fantastic. The last hostess just had a baby and isn't coming back, so that will work out amazingly. It's just four shifts a week but there's room for more. And if you like it, you could always end up being a waitress."

"That's great. I don't have any experience as a waitress, so starting as a hostess would be really good," I tell her.

"Okay, also, here's my number. And let me know if you have any other questions. Otherwise, I'll see you at noon on Monday."

"Perfect," I say, feeling lighter when I leave than when I came.

Lemon and Plum already went back to her house and so I pull out my phone to call Bartlett and let him know where I am when I realize he's probably already back at the hardware store.

I take a right to go around the corner when someone tugs on my wrist. I pull in a sharp breath, caught off guard, knowing Bartlett would never touch me so roughly because even though his last name suggests otherwise, he's the most gentle man I've ever met.

"There you are," my father, Baron, hisses. "You are one hard person to track down."

My eyes narrow. "Let go of me," I shout as he drags me into the alley behind the brewery. "Let go of me, Dad."

His truck is behind the brewery. My heart falls, realizing the circus semis may have headed to Burly, but my father and Ricky stayed behind, determined to find me.

Ricky jumps out of the truck when he sees me. "You have no idea how pissed I am at you. You're supposed to be mine," he growls. "Mine. Your dad promised you to me and you knew that good and well."

"I'm neither of yours," I say, knowing the last thing I want is to return to a life with these two men. Men who kept me caged. After falling for Bartlett, I know what it means to be free – to be accepted and seen for who I am – and I can't go back to this. To them.

"Well, that's what you think," Ricky laughs.

"Let go of me!" I shout at my father.

Ricky reaches for the gun at his hip. Then points it to my back. "We don't have a show without you, which means you're coming with us."

13

BARTLETT

LEMON CALLS as we leave the police station.

"Hey," she says. "So, Abby went to an interview at Home Brew. Plum and I are back at my house. I just wanted to give you the 411; that's where she's at."

"You left her there?" I say. "Lemon!"

"She's fine. She's with Griffin."

"I know, but how long ago was that? What if the interview's over?"

"You think she could be in that much trouble?" Lemon asks. "I'm sorry, I didn't realize it was that serious."

I need to get to Home Brew. I need to get there now, already rushing down the street, Reuben next to me.

"The thing is, Lemon, Graham's patrol guys saw

some big trucks and semis come in about an hour ago with the Big Top Circus logo on the side headed to the Burly Fairgrounds, but one of the trucks split." Fuck. I need to find my girl.

"Shit," Ruben says. "Griffin's outside. She's not with Abby."

We stop Griffin outside of the brewery, asking where Abby went.

"She just left here a few minutes ago. Sorry, was she supposed to go somewhere else?" Griffin shakes her head, frowning, confused.

"Do you know which way she went?"

"Honestly, I have no idea," Griffin says. "I was too preoccupied with getting these menu boards out for tonight's specials."

Ruben helps her set the signage up on the side-walk, but I'm already pushing past them. "Sorry," I say. "I just got to find her."

There's a shout, a scream.

"That's her," I say, "goddammit."

Griffin's eyes are knitted with worry and Reuben follows me as we round the corner toward the alley. I hear Rueben on the phone with Rye, who is coming around Warm Way just as we are coming from the other direction.

"I was at the bakery," he says. He's holding a croissant. He drops it in a trash can as he joins us, our eyes locked. "Abby?" he says.

I nod. "She's in trouble," I say it as a truck drives off down the alley. "I know she's in there," I say.

I run down the alley after it, but I can't see her. Can't see anyone.

"Goddammit," I shout.

But my truck is right next door in the alley behind Hammer Home.

I jump in, my brothers with me: Rueben in the truck bed, Rye at my side. I tail the truck, my foot on the gas, driving fast as I can.

A moment later, the truck that I know Abby's in jolts to a halt, and I'm about to rear-end it. Then it turns down Restful Road.

"Shit, Bart," Rye says. "I should have never questioned her or how you care her about her or anything. You knew what you were doing."

"You want to do this now?" I ask. "When we're in the middle of a car chase?"

"We're gonna get her, okay?" Rye's words are firm. Resolute. "No matter what, we're gonna get her."

He's right, of course. We are. Because we're not gonna let anybody, and I mean anybody, hurt the woman I love.

He's calling our other brother, Mac. "Hey," Rye says. "Where are you?"

"Grabbing some pizza at Home Slice."

"You have your car?"

"Yeah, why?"

"Get in it now. I need you to turn onto Restful Road and I need you to block the red pickup truck that's going to be headed your way in about two minutes. Understood?"

"All right," Mac says, ending the call.

I look over at Rye. "Thanks."

Ruben shoves open the window in the back of my truck. "What's the hold up? Where's your girl? We need to rear-end this truck in front of us. You understand?"

"I'm on it," I say just as I see Mac's truck coming toward us on the other side of the road.

"Now, you just gotta sandwich that truck," Rye insists, calling Graham as I maneuver the truck on the road.

"Just?" I shake my head, swearing under my breath.

"Yes," Rye snorts, "*just*. Punch the gas."

I do as he says, and the truck ahead of us does the same, but it can't get very far because Mac, being the youngest brother, T's his car in front of the truck and I do the same with mine.

We've blocked Restful Road entirely, but we've also barricaded the truck.

All four of us Rough boys jump out of our vehicles and surround it.

"Get out of the car," I shout. "Now!"

A man who's big, and I mean really fucking big, gets out. "Don't talk to me like that. I'm Ricky, the strongest man in the world."

Mac's eyes widen. "You got to be kidding me."

"They're in the circus," Rye grunts, "what do you expect?"

I'm not laughing, though, because none of this is funny. This is Abby we're talking about.

"Where is she?" I say as another man, I'm guessing Abby's father, drags her out from the truck. She's crying, shaking, scared. This girl, this woman I love, is terrified. And I see why, Ricky's got a gun pointed at her.

"He's gonna shoot if you don't back down, you understand me? I'm her father. I know what's best. And what's best is her coming with me. Now!"

"What's this about?" I shout. "You just want some power and control over your child? Well, you lost it. She's a grown woman and she can decide what she wants."

"What she wants? This girl never knew a thing about what she wanted. She just bent over backwards and did what I said her whole damn life."

"Well, she's not bending anymore. She's standing up straight now," I say, my voice loud, clear, strong. I may have been doing what I was told my whole life too, but right now, I'm doing what matters. And that's protecting the woman I love.

I'm lined up with all four of my brothers and we all know what we've got to do.

We've got to disarm this man and we've got to get Abby back.

She belongs to us now. She's as rough as we are.

Her eyes find mine and I swear to God, her soul and mine, they're one. I'm gonna do what I have to, even if it means taking a damn bullet for her. Because this woman, she's my woman. And even if the strongest man in the world is between us, he's not gonna keep us apart.

"I want to do something stupid," I tell Ricky. "Like fight you for her honor," I say. "I want to challenge you to some competition and the winner takes all. But I'm not gonna do something that dumb because Abby is worth so much more than one wrestling match or one fight."

"You're just scared!" he shouts at me.

"No. Abby, she's worth everything. And if you think that gun is going to keep her locked in a cage forever then you know nothing about that woman. Because she may have been a caged bird for 21 years, but she's had a taste of freedom and her wings aren't clipped anymore."

I walk straight up to him. "You need to drop your gun," I say, "and you need to drop it now."

Abby shakes her head. "He'll shoot you," she says. "Don't do something you're gonna regret. Don't do it for me."

"Don't do something I would regret?" I say. "Not fighting for you, that would be the regret."

"Get away from her," her father shouts. "She's not yours."

"Well, she's not yours either," I say. "She's her own person."

Just then, Rye rushes forward. Rueben and Mac dive too. I grin, realizing what they're doing: creating a fucking distraction. They all shout, screaming at the same time, "Drop the gun!"

It scares Ricky because he didn't see it coming. These three Rough men diving, rolling in the middle of the road toward him. Reuben wraps an arm around his neck. Mac reaches for a wrist. Rye, though, is the one who is attempting to disarm him. And when he does, Ricky moves his hand. And while the gun is no longer pointed at Abby, it's suddenly pointed at me.

I try to roll away, to dodge the goddamn bullet, but it clips my shoulder. As it hits me, I fall to the ground, the burst of pain blinding me as my knees buckle. As my hand instinctively presses to my shoulder, blood saturates my hand. Ricky's bullet hit me.

Rye takes action, making sure Ricky's hands are

behind his back. He's taken to the ground by all four of my brothers and he's sure as hell not going anywhere.

Abby, she runs to me, wrapping her arms around me. And for a moment, I think her father is going to get away scot-free, but Mac realizes that at the exact same time. They jump that old man the same way we demolish my mother's Thanksgiving dinner: fast and furious.

Abby kisses me, her hands on my cheeks. "Oh my God. We have to get you to the hospital. I can't believe Ricky shot you."

We hear the roar of the sirens. Graham is here arresting and handcuffing both the men and I'm loaded onto a gurney. Abby's crying as she realizes what's happening.

"I'm just going down the block," I tell her. "And it's a shoulder wound. I'll be fine. Hell, you hardly complained when this happened to you."

"You were hit by a bullet. It's a lot worse than what happened to me."

"Hey, speaking of," Graham calls out, "we just found those thugs, that was what took us so damn long to get here. They jumped another girl in Burly." Then he grins. "Ha, funnily enough, which I know, Abby, it might be a bit too soon to joke about, your father and this man might be sharing a cell tonight with those fools who thought they were gonna have a piece of you."

"Me showing up in this town caused a lot of trouble," she says.

I shake my head, taking her hand. If I'm going in this ambulance, this woman is coming with me. "No," I tell her, "you showing up in this town means you came home. You came home for good."

14

ABBY

ONE WEEK LATER...

SINCE PLUM DIDN'T GET her circus trip last week, she asked if everyone would come with a circus act before Sunday dinner. We all agreed because telling Plum no is out of the question. Not because we're wrapped around her a little finger, but well, okay, scratch that. Every single member of the Rough family is wrapped around this five-year-old's finger with good reason.

Not only is she adorable and sweet as can be, but she is also full of curiosity and there is something special in that. Something nobody wants her to lose anytime soon. Especially me.

My life has not been charmed like Plum's is.

And I know she has had her fair share of loss, but there's a magic to her right now. Her eyes sparkle as she takes in her whole family here, setting up her circus. I am not sure what acts everyone is going to be performing, but everyone has been willing to play their part. Even her Grandpa Red is the circus master. He found a top hat and he's using Hijinx as his tiger.

I smile as I watch everyone gather around the front yard. Dinner's at 6:00, but we arrived at 3:00 so we could set up the circus for Plum. Even her great grandparents, Rosie and Reynold, have come out to see the show, which I think is pretty sweet. And her Great Uncle Filson and Great Aunt Ruby are here as well. The legendary Rowdy boys haven't come, but that's because they weren't invited.

When I asked Bartlett why they weren't allowed to come, he said, "No way. This is a kid's show. Those boys are way too wild for a circus set for a five-year-old."

Not understanding what that meant, I dropped it and focused instead on making sure my act wasn't going to be a mess. I haven't walked a tightrope in quite a while, and I've never performed for an audience that meant so much to me.

"Ladies and gentlemen," Redford Rough calls,

gathering his family around to the front porch. Everyone is sitting on blankets or Adirondack chairs or on the steps of the big, wide, porch. "I would like to welcome you to the first ever Rough Family Circus, not to be confused with our traditional Thanksgiving Rough Family Talent Show."

I look over at Lemon. "You guys have a family talent show?"

She nods. "Oh yes. Thanksgiving tradition, and you cannot skip a performance."

"Good to know," I say, smiling, laughing really, and wondering if I'll be lucky enough to share Thanksgiving with this family one day. I'm not one who makes risky bets, but God, I would go all in with these people because they are the only family I want.

I smile as Red welcomes the first act of the evening. "Ladies and gentlemen, I would like to introduce the magical, the alluring, the sensational, The Real Mac-aroni."

Mac walks up from where he was sitting on an old stump. He has an ax slung over his shoulder and a log under his arm. "I am going to dazzle with acts of bravery, acts of strength, acts of–"

Plum starts giggling loudly, and Mac can't help but grin, breaking his acting bravado. "I'm the strongest man in the world," he says, showing us his muscles, which there are a lot of. Then he sets the log down on his stump and he swings that ax, slicing through the log as everyone in the family cheers, laughing hard, hollering and hooting as he lifts the ax overhead in a victory dance.

Red calls the next act forward. "Now, it's time to see our performer who travels far and wide. You may know her as the elusive, as the marvelous, as the magical Lemonada."

Lemon stands, and somehow, she has found a turban and a tasseled shawl, wrapped around her as she sashays before us all. "Hello, my darlings," she says with a dramatic accent. "I would like to read someone's palm to find their fortune." She walks over to Rye. "May I have the privilege of taking your hand and reading your love line?"

Everyone laughs riotously because the idea of Rye falling in love is ridiculous. He plays along though, knowing Plum is watching every move. He gives her a smile and Plum skips over, climbing into her grumpy uncle's lap.

"How do you read palms, Auntie Lemon?" she asks.

"You must look ever so carefully at this line here. But there's a tragedy in your future, Rye. Look," she says, pointing dramatically to the center of Rye's hand as Plum's eyes widen in shock and glee. "His line cuts into two, which means–"

Plum shrieks. "What does it mean? What does

it mean?"

"It means he must make a choice or he will never love at all."

Rye rolls his eyes and Plum laughs, jumping out of her uncle's lap as Red takes the center of the yard once again. "Okay, now that we have that figured out, let's see what the next act is. Who do we have? We have Graham Cracker," Red says, and he points to the right, where we see Graham riding a unicycle very, very poorly through the grass toward us until he falls off very, very dramatically.

"Okay, so that act needs work," Red says as Graham clutches his belly in laughter. Next up, Fig knots a cherry stem with her tongue, which has her father grumbling and her brothers shouting at her – *you better not be doing anything like that with any boys from town.*

And then Annie brings out some apples and shows us her juggling skills. Plum does a hula hoop routine. And Rueben shows us a magic trick in which he disappears, goes into the house, and returns with a can of beer.

"That's not a magic trick," Bartlett jokes. "That's you going into the house and getting some Rainier. And you didn't even bring me one."

Reuben laughs. "Well, I guess you need to work on your act. Speaking of, what's your act?"

"Hey, hey, hey," I say, standing. "Me first."

Redford nods. "Exactly. The lady goes first."

I already have my slackline ready between the two trees behind Red. He helped me put it up earlier today. "Okay, I'm a little nervous," I say, walking to the tree to the left. The line is about twelve feet in the air, and Red helps me with a ladder.

I climb it and Bartlett immediately begins to shake his head. "You can't go up there."

"I can," I say. "In fact, I could do this about 30 feet in the air. The show must go on, Bart! This is Plum's circus."

Plum smiles. "Can you really tightrope walk?"

"Sure thing, kiddo," I say.

I begin to walk across the slackline between the two tall trees. Red is beneath me. I know he's doing it in a fatherly way, thinking he'll catch me if I fall. And Bartlett is suddenly underneath me too, though his shoulder is still bandaged from the bullet he took for me.

And honestly, I'm not going to tell them that if I fall from here, it's going to be so fast that they won't have time to catch me. Right now, Bartlett just wants to believe he would, and that is enough.

The thing is, I'm not going to fall. I can do this.

I walk the slackline once and then twice, and then I jump off of it, landing in a headstand. Then I do four cartwheels toward Plum, landing in a perfect split. Then I do a backhanded jump. I land in a handspring, place a few more cartwheels, and then I do a pirouette right in front of her.

"Happy Circus Day," I tell her, and everyone stands, giving me an ovation I do not deserve. "Stop it," I say, blushing.

Fig is gobsmacked. "Abby, you said you were a gymnast. You are freaking amazing."

Annie nods in agreement. "You really are incredible. Have you ever thought of opening a gymnastics studio? The kids in Home would love something like that. You know, there's an open building right next to the toy store."

"I've been there," I say. "Bartlett took me to Home Grown for dinner."

"Ooh, fancy," Annie says. "I'm impressed, Bart."

"But yeah, that would be pretty incredible to have a little studio," I say, remembering the leotards hanging in the sports store that day when I met Harold and I got my phone charger. I smile, an idea coming to me. "Actually, I could call it Rough and Tumble. What do you think?"

The family all laughs, smiling in agreement. "That would be perfect," Bartlett says. "I mean, if you were a Rough."

There's an awkward silence, and I realize I may have just put my foot in my mouth, claiming the Rough name when I'm not a Rough at all.

But then Bartlett gives me a grin. "Hey Dad, is it time for my act?"

"Of course, son. I think it's the perfect time."

"Well, you mentioned Rough and Tumble, right? And then I said that awkward thing there about you not being a Rough," Bart says, grinning sheepishly.

"Right," I say, cringing. "I'm kind of mortified actually."

"Well, the thing is, I was hoping you would be. Not mortified. A Rough."

"What do you mean?" I ask, looking around at his whole family. They're all watching. Plum is right by my side. Her eyes, they still sparkle. Fig and Lemon, there's tears in theirs that they're blinking back. Annie's too. "What's going on?" I ask.

And then Bartlett is on one knee and I see that everyone is in on this.

This whole moment? It was made for me.

"I love you, Abracadabra. And I want to be your husband. I know you came to this town when you were a little girl and it meant something to you then. And you came back here because you were looking for that feeling. You were looking for that memory. And the thing is, I'm so happy you did because you coming Home means I found *my home*. I may have grown up here with this perfect family and this perfect life, but what if I had grown old without you?

"Marry me. Be my family. Be my forever. And have that studio called Rough and Tumble. And I'm guessing we'll have some rough and tumble times. But Abby, I think we can get through them, any of them, together. What do you say?" he asks, pulling out a diamond ring and offering it to me. "Will you be my wife?"

Tears fall down my cheeks; my heart bursts with devotion. My whole body hums with hope. "I love you, Bartlett. I didn't think a girl like me could ever be paired with a man like you, but somehow you proved me wrong. You won me over, and you made me yours."

"Is that a yes?" Annie asks on behalf of her whole family.

"That's a yes," I say as Bartlett slides the ring on my finger and stands, wrapping me up in his arms and kissing me hard on the lips.

His eyes find mine and his hands are on my cheeks. "I love you, Abby. I'm sorry I just told everyone your real name."

"I don't care," I say, laughing. "The only thing I care about is you and me, us."

Plum is clapping. "That was the best circus finale in the whole wide world," she says, and I laugh. She's right, this was the best show on earth.

EPILOGUE

BARTLETT

ONE MONTH LATER...

MOST GIRLS MIGHT NOT WANT to get married in a barn, but Abby's not most girls, and this isn't any regular barn.

It's a hundred years old and it's been updated quite a few times. A few decades ago, my dad put in pine floors, insulated windows, and electricity. It's heated now, and it's a better venue than anywhere they've got down in town.

Besides, it's nestled in the woods here on our family's land in our mountains. I don't think there's any finer place to get hitched. And the fact that my bride-to-be thought the same thing, well, it warms my goddamn heart.

"You ready for this?" Rye asks.

My brothers are surrounding me, and Rye looks at me like I'm a fool, but that's only because he hasn't met a woman who changed his goddamn life.

I feel sorry for the man, if I'm being honest, because meeting Abby made my world so much better, so much brighter, and Rye hasn't had that pleasure yet. "More than ready," I say. "This is going to be a good fucking day."

"Yeah, I bet you'll be fucking, all right," Graham says, joking.

"Hey," I growl. "Don't talk about my wedding night like that."

The boys get the picture. And besides, my father and my grandfather are walking over with silver flasks of whiskey. "Do you need a strong drink before you say I do?" my dad asks.

I take a pull on what he offers because it seems like a gentlemanly thing to do, and my grandfather slips me an envelope.

"Something for a nest egg," he says. "Congratulations, grandson. I'm really proud of you."

"Thanks, Gramps," I say, appreciating Grandpa Reynolds in ways he may never understand. His integrity and honor are part of the reason us boys are all standing here today.

He taught my father what it meant to be a real man. And my father showed us boys what that meant too. And now, well, now I'm ready to really man up and become a husband. Abby's husband. Damn. I think it's time.

Everyone I know and love in town is here. My Rowdy cousins from Burly have come, and my other grandpa, Crockett, is here. My Uncle Angus showed up too. Somehow most of them are in ties and suit coats to boot. Though I know my mother had plenty to do with that. Their mama, my aunt Dolly who died a long time ago, was my mom's best friend and ended up her sister-in-law. Now, Mom makes it her mission to make sure the Rowdy boys are looked after to some degree, in respect for Dolly. I know if my aunt Dolly were alive, she'd be the one singing at my wedding today because she had the voice of an angel, and everyone in this town knew it.

Well, the Rowdy boys may be in suits and ties, but they're wearing their cowboy boots – which I'm sure would actually make their mama proud, truth be told. I smile, shaking their hands, all of us clapping one another on the backs.

And then it's time to walk my mother down the aisle. We have a local harpist playing in the corner. There are flowers everywhere. I don't even know where Fig and Lemon and Abby found so many flowers in February, but they did. And everything's red and pink and white because, well, it's February 14th. Somehow I'm getting married on the most romantic day of the year, which, well, Abby wanted it so I was going to give it to her.

"You look so handsome, Bart," my mom says, holding my hand as I walk her down the aisle.

"Well, you look pretty beautiful yourself, Mom," I say.

"You know, I didn't think you'd get swept off your feet so fast. You were always the sensible brother. You know that? But..."

"What?" I ask.

"You also are a momma's boy."

"Is that a bad thing?"

"No," she says. "It means you're sensitive in ways your other brothers aren't. And it means Abby's really lucky to have you, Bartlett."

When we reach her seat, I give my mom a big old hug. I kiss her cheek and I tell her how much I love her. "So damn much," I say.

"I love you too, sweetheart. Now go make me proud."

"I will," I tell her.

I take my place next to Pastor Andy, and I watch as my sisters walk down the aisle.

I decided not to have any groomsmen because, well, they were all going to be groomsmen – all those brothers of mine. So I figured we'd keep it simple. The girls wanted a chance to wear pretty dresses, and so we decided to give them that.

But the real showstopper, the real reason we're here, well, besides the cake and the champagne and the dancing that's going to come later and the wedding night that's going to come after that, is so we can see Abby as she walks down the aisle.

Her dress is long, white, satin, strapless, and designed by Fig. Abby had one request, that she could dance in it. God, I can't wait to spin my wife around the dance floor of this barn.

When she comes down the aisle, everyone turns, everyone stands, and they look at the most beautiful woman in the room. And she is. Abra-cadabra. She is a sight to be seen. My heart skips about a dozen beats and my eyes, they well up with tears. And when I take a good, hard look at her, I know like I knew before – she's the one for me. She makes me feel alive and known and seen. Like I'm home.

I watch her take those steps down the aisle, holding that bouquet of pink and red roses, thinking she looks so delicate and loving that for her because I know for a woman who's been through so many hard times, the chance to feel soft, to feel special, means a whole awful lot.

She hands the roses to Fig and takes her place beside me. Her hands are in my hands, and her heart, well, I'm holding it tight too. Pastor Andy asks us to recite our vows, *to have and to hold from this day forward, through sickness and in health.*

The words are easy to say. The promises are ones I know I can keep because Abby, she's my wife. She's my best friend and she's my forever.

"I do," she says.

"I do," I repeat.

"I now pronounce you husband and wife," Pastor Andy says. "You may kiss the bride."

And when I step toward her and her mouth meets mine, it's more than a kiss. It's the beginning of a life.

Afterwards, we dance in that big red barn. The music now isn't a harp. It's a big old band, and everyone's having a hooting and hollering time. My cousins, Cash and Williams especially, are getting down.

Abby asks if this is everything I imagined. "It's more than I imagined," I tell her. "It's everything. And what about you? You're the bride."

She laughs. "This is beyond my wildest dreams. But you know we still have our wedding night. And I've had plenty of dreams about that too."

"Now have you?" I ask, holding my girl ever so tightly, kissing her again, hard.

My cousin Cash whistles, and Abby laughs. "Oh my God. Those Rowdy boys really are rowdy. They think they're at a party, not a wedding."

"You want me to go Rough 'em up?"

"No, I don't want you to go rough them up, but maybe you need to go rough up Rye."

We look over at my brother in the corner. He's drinking a beer, growling about something.

"You think Rye has a chance of ever being happy?" Abby asks.

"You want to know what I heard?"

She nods as I swing her around the dance floor. "My father is about to send him off to our old family hunting cabin in the Rough Valley."

"Really?"

"Yeah. I heard him talking to Grandpa Reynolds before the wedding, saying if Rye doesn't snap out of it, he's going to send him to the cabin to clear his head because he is in one bad mood."

"You mean like send him out to the sticks alone and tell him not to come back until he's able to be nice?"

"I don't know. Look, he looks like he's going to argue with anyone who gets too close. He needs someone to soften him up."

"Or screw him silly," Abby says.

"I like what you're thinking." I give her another kiss, more than ever ready to drag her out of this place altogether.

Soon enough, I can. And I do.

We make our way to the Home Away From Home Bed and Breakfast. Hijinx is happily spending some time with Plum and Rueben while we're away in Hawaii for our honeymoon next week. But before we can get to the warm, sunny beaches of Maui, we have one night here together.

"Funny, if I had been able to stay at this bed and breakfast that first night in town, maybe I would've never ended up with you," Abby says as we enter the quiet lodgings.

Mary hands us our keys without another word, knowing this night is ours. She looks away, probably not wanting to think about what's going to happen next. I appreciate her discretion and realize she's probably had to do a lot of looking away over the years, managing a hotel.

"I think I would've ended up with you no matter what, Abby. You and me, we are a perfect pair. Remember?"

"Oh, I remember," she says as I scoop her up from the floor and carry her to our room, unlocking the door and carrying her past the threshold to the bed. She laughs as I move on top of her, toward her, into her, filling her, taking her. "Oh my God," she moans.

Naked before me, my bride wears nothing except a veil in her hair. "You look so beautiful," I tell her. "Head to toe perfection."

She runs a hand over the scar on my shoulder where the bullet met my bone. "I love you so much, Bartlett," she tells me, wrapping her arms around my neck, her naked body against my naked body, her skin, my skin.

We move as one to the bed, my lips on hers, kissing her deeply, knowing that this night is one I will never forget.

She is my memories from here on out.

We move together, her body linked for eternity with mine.

I touch her, fingering her and licking her and making her wet, making her moan and making her happy in a way she deserves.

My cock aches to fill her again and again. And she eagerly offers me everything she has.

"Don't stop," she whimpers.

"I'll never stop," I promise, touching her again, easing her open, my cock centering right where it belongs.

Our fingers lace, her eyes on me. "I love you," she says again.

"I'm so glad you made it Home," I tell her.

Order Now

ROUGH DEAL: Coming Home to the Mountain Book 2

Everyone has a secret.

Mine is ruining my life... making me bitter, callous, cold.

I'm Rye Rough – the oldest of seven kids with a family tree that built this town. I understand more than most that reputations matter.

Which is why I keep my mouth shut – and that secret? I'm not telling a soul.

Working as my dad's right-hand man, I'm angrier than ever – and hell, it's messing with the family construction company.

My father forces a deal: Go to the rural family cabin and don't come back until I get my head on straight or I lose my place in the business.

As if spending more time alone is going to solve anything.

One day into my retreat, I find Prairie, a beautifully fragile woman who is lost, alone, and in need of my tender loving care. Her life has been one of confinement and abuse.

She needs me like I've never been needed before.

My family doesn't understand my love for her.

My secret keeps me up at night.

Something must give before it all breaks.

One thing is sure – rough hands have been dealt for both Prairie and me ... and for our love to survive, we can't fold.

Chapter 1

Rye

It hasn't always been like this.

I used to come home for Sunday dinner and enjoy myself. Sit at the table, watch my family, shoot the shit, and think how good I had it. Think how lucky I was to be the oldest of seven siblings, living up here on Rough Mountain, my family the ones who built this town of Home, Washington.

As my father's go-to man with the world in the palm of my hand, I had the respect of anyone I wanted. Hell, I built a home of my own by the time I was twenty-two years old.

Far as anyone could tell, I had it made.

Then one year ago, everything fucking changed.

"WOULD YOU LIKE ANOTHER SERVING?" Mom asks, bringing me back to the present. Those bad memories are pushed aside as she hands me a platter of her chicken. She's sitting next to me at the table, trying to fatten me up, thinking maybe if I get some more meat on my bones, I might become happier. Smile more often. I know she's worried. Everyone here is worried.

"Thanks, Mom," I say, adding another chicken thigh to my already heaping plate of food. My mom has a few love languages. One of them is feeding her kids until they're more than full. I would never resist my mother's home-cooked meals.

She smiles at me softly but she looks tired. Like she needs a break. And hell, I'm sure she does.

Fig, the youngest of us Rough kids, is in the

second semester of her senior year of high school and giving my mother a run for her money. You'd think by the end of raising all seven kids she would have this down pat, but Fig is like none of the rest of us. Wild in ways I wasn't. Which is saying something considering I know I've been a handful.

"How's work going?" Mom asks me.

Work is the last thing I want to talk about.

The table is full and loud. Mac and Graham are arguing as usual. Fig and Lemon are discussing the dress Fig is planning to wear to some school dance. Bartlett is staring at his new bride, Abby.

Plum is looking at her grandpa Red like he's the greatest man on earth which, well, in her eyes, he is. Rueben, Plum's dad, is in the other room on a call and I'm wondering what that's all about, but I'm not rude enough to ask. Even though everyone at this table thinks I've turned into an asshole.

But there's all different kinds of assholes. Me? I'm just rubbing everyone the wrong way. It doesn't mean I don't know how to be polite.

And I hope it means Reuben is talking to some woman. God knows he deserves to be happy after the hell he and Plum have gone through.

Mom nudges me. "How are you doing? I tried calling this week and never heard back. You busy with work?"

"Work is going fine, Mom."

"Is it?" she asks, taking a bite of her green salad. "Because your father said things haven't been going so great at the lodge build site."

I scowl, feeling like shit for bringing trouble to my mother's life. That's the last thing she needs. "Well, you don't need to worry, Mom. It's all good."

"Since when have you fought with the newer guys on the crew?" Mom presses. "Used to keep to yourself if you were unhappy, now you seem set on making everyone around you miserable."

"Annie," Dad says softly from across the table. He never has to speak loudly to get her attention. I swear they have a secret language. "Maybe we should have a family meeting if we are going to go *there*."

Mom nods. "You're right, Red. We should. We all need to clear the air. I only see Rye once a week. When else am I supposed to talk to him? God knows he won't come over any other time unless it's a family obligation."

Across the table I hear Lemon scoff. "Yeah, when you don't come around, it means we pick up your slack."

I run a hand over my beard, annoyed at the sudden shift in conversation. "Point taken, Lemon. Anyone else have something they wanna say? Family meeting can begin. Say whatever you want."

All our lives, if there was something that needed to be said, my parents let us go for it—they preferred us talking it out, even if it felt harsh, rather than leaving things to simmer under the surface.

Unfortunately, right now, everything I feel inside is about ready to boil over.

"Yeah, matter of fact I do have a few more things to say to you," Lemon tosses back, sour as ever. "Why are you so mad at us? What did we do to you?"

I balk looking at her, unable to answer. If I do, it will only make this worse. But me keeping my mouth shut pisses her off something fierce.

She rolls her eyes. We've always been fire and ice, oil and vinegar.

This is no exception.

Mac clears his throat, not meeting my eyes. "Dad needs you on the crew, Rye, with your head on straight. He counts on you. And you're making things hard for us at work. The guys were mad on Friday with you hollering about—"

"Hey," Bartlett says, cutting Mac off, always the peacemaker. "We don't need to do this. I'm sure Rye is just having a rough time, but everything will work out. Let's just eat this amazing food Mom made—"

Graham chuckles. As the brother who's right in

the middle, he always seems to find situations funny even when they should be taken more seriously.

"What are you laughing about?" Mac asks him.

Graham groans. "I just think it's funny. Bartlett always wants to put Rye in his place. But Bart's not the oldest. Rye is."

Mac drops his fork. "Well, if Rye wants to be the oldest, why doesn't he start acting like it?"

"Hey," Reuben says, off his phone call, stepping in and taking Plum's hand. "We're going to take Hijinx out for a walk, that okay, Abby?"

Abby looks over and smiles at Reuben. "Sounds good. Thanks, Plum."

The adults in the room understand that Reuben is doing his fatherly duty of getting his daughter out of this grown-up conversation, which is really more of a fight.

Part of me wishes Reuben would stay. He's the brother who's usually on my side. But he always puts his daughter first. Because he's a Rough. He knows what really matters—family.

I know what matters too.

That's why I have this secret. Why I have this problem.

Why everyone at the table thinks I'm a goddamn asshole when really, I'm trying to protect them.

Family comes first.

The last thing I want to do is ruin them by telling them the truth.

"I don't know what you want from me," I say, defeated. "Just tell me what you want."

Fig opens her mouth. "I want you to stop being so grumpy. Be the brother I remember. The one who laughed at dinner, who came over just because and told stories all night at the fire pit. I miss him."

"It's like we're walking on eggshells," Lemon says softly.

"And it's exhausting, Rye," Fig says with a half-laugh.

There's a few chuckles at that comment—at the moment, her teenage antics are a bit exhausting themselves. Fig just rolls her eyes, crossing her arms.

"Hey," Graham says, winking at our little sister. "Don't laugh at Fig for speaking her truth. Even if she's her usual drama queen." I know he is trying to lighten the mood—but it's too late.

"Well, *I'm exhausted* by this family meeting," I tell everyone at the table.

I take my plate and carry it into the kitchen. Wanting to be done with this night—done with all of it. Clearly no one in this family is happy with me or the way I've been acting and handling things.

Point taken. Understood. I'll go home now and get out of their goddamn hair.

My father, though, meets me in the kitchen. "Son."

"What?" I turn to him. "You know, I really didn't appreciate that blindside. If you were upset with the way work was going, you could have talked to me."

"We are all worried about you."

"I don't know if it was worry in people's voices or if everyone's just sick and tired of me," I say.

"I think people are sick and tired of you too," Dad says with a teasing chuckle, running a hand through his beard. "Rye, I don't know what's going on with you. But these last few months, hell, this last year, you're not yourself. I'm worried about you, son."

"Are you?" I ask.

"Ever since Luke died..." Dad shakes his head, missing his best friend. "I know the business has changed with him gone. And maybe I put too much on your plate. Maybe I expected too much."

"No, that's not it. That's not it *at all*," I repeat more intensely. I reach for my keys on the counter. Grab my jacket on the back of a kitchen chair. "I'm leaving," I say. "I'll see you at the site tomorrow."

"No," Dad says, "actually, you won't."

"What are you trying to say?" I ask my father. We've been working side by side for the last decade. Ever since I graduated high school I've been working on his crew, until I started *leading* his crew.

"I'm saying it's time for you to leave town for a bit right now. You got to figure out your shit before you come back to the job site and before you come back to family dinner. Before you come back Home."

"You're kicking me out of town?"

"Yeah," Dad says. "I am. You need to go to the Rough Forest. Go to the family hunting cabin."

I give a sharp laugh. "You want me to go to the middle of bumfuck nowhere? Is there even running water out there? It's fucking February."

"It'll be March first in a week," he says, "you'll be fine. And yeah, there's water. There's a well up there."

"Has anyone in the family been there in the last few years?" I ask.

"I'm not sure," Dad says, "why don't you go up there and find out. Pack your truck and head up to the mountains."

"We're already living in the mountains," I tell him.

"I'm talking about the real mountains. You go to

the Rough Forest and clear your head, son. You come home when you're ready to be a real family man."

"You say it like it's an ultimatum or something."

"No, it's a deal."

"It doesn't seem like much of a deal," I say, angry that the secret I am keeping to protect him is hurting me more than ever. "I don't really see what say I have in this."

"The deal is this, son: you go up there and clear your head or you're not coming back to my job site."

"Oh, it's your job site now? I thought it was our family business."

"It's my business until the day I die. Rye, I always hoped one day I would give it to you. But I'm not handing my business over to a man who is this unhappy. You need to remember what it means to be alive."

He understands nothing. I'm holding secrets inside to protect him.

I walk past him without saying goodbye to the rest of my family because I already know what they're thinking. They're sick of me.

And I'm not going to change their minds with anything I say right now. My head's too hot. My body is all tense, feeling ready to throw down.

Since I'm not going to start a fight with my flesh

and blood, I know it's better for me to just get the hell out of Dodge.

Order Now

ABOUT THE AUTHOR

Frankie Love writes filthy-sweet stories about bad boys and mountain men.
Frankie is ridiculously in love with her own bearded hottie, believes in love-at-first-sight, and happily-ever-afters. She also believes in the power of a quickie.

Find Frankie here:
www.frankielove.net
frankieloveromance@gmail.com